KATE RYDER

KATE RYDER

by Hester Burton

illustrated by Victor G. Ambrus

❧

Thomas Y. Crowell Company

New York

Originally published in Great Britain under the title *Kate Rider*
First United States Publication 1975
Copyright © 1974 by Hester Burton

Library of Congress Cataloging in Publication Data

Burton, Hester. Kate Ryder.
Summary: In 1646 a young English girl tries to cope with the many pressures, changes, and divided loyalties that the continuing Civil War imposes upon her family.
 1. Great Britain—History—Civil War, 1642–1651—Juv. fiction. [1. Great Britain —History—Civil War, 1642–1651—Fiction] I. Ambrus, Victor G., ill. II. Title.
PZ7.B953Kat [Fic] 75-8576 ISBN 0-690-00978-X

1 2 3 4 5 6 7 8 9 10

For Ann Beneduce

~ Contents ~

❧ *Note on the English Civil War*

Some readers may not be familiar with the historical events which form the background of this story. The English Civil War (1642–1651) was the outcome of a long-standing quarrel between the King and Parliament over the extent to which Parliament should share in the government of the country. When Parliament, in 1641, demanded wide constitutional changes and the raising of an army controlled by Parliament and not by the King, King Charles I refused to agree and, in the following year, gathered a small army of his own to challenge Parliament's power. Civil warfare broke out.

The King's men were called Royalists or Cavaliers; their opponents Roundheads (because they cut their hair short), Puritans, or Parliament men. Most of King Charles' support came from great landowners and their tenants, including the Roman Catholic minority, in the North and West of the country. The greatest strength of Parliament was in the eastern counties (for example in Norfolk, Suffolk, Essex, and Kent) in the South and in London, among merchants, smaller landowners, and yeoman farmers (such as John Ryder). Many of these were Puritan in religion. But there was no exact geographical or social division.

By the summer of 1646, when the story of *Kate Ryder* begins, the Royalist armies have been virtually defeated in the field. The long war appears to be almost at an end. But in the next two years, encouraged by their enemies' quarreling among themselves, the King's supporters make another bid for power, rising to fight their cause not only in Scotland and Wales but also in Puritan Kent and Essex. It is with the fortunes of the Royalist army in the east under its general, Lord Goring, and its final defeat in the siege of Colchester by the Parliament armies under their great general, Thomas Fairfax, that the story of *Kate Ryder* comes to a close.

CAMBRIDGESHIRE

SUFFOLK

BURY
St. EDMUNDS

HADLEIGH

RIVER COLNE

STRATFORD

HERTFORDSHIRE

HALSTEAD

MANNINGTREE

COGGESHALL COLCHESTER

TO
NORTH
SEA

BRAINTREE

ESSEX

ST. OSYTH

CHELMSFORD

BRENTWOOD

BOW

LONDON

GREENWICH

R. THAMES

RIVER THAMES

ISLE OF
DOGS

ROCHESTER

CANTERBURY

KENT

High Ashfield, 1646

1

Kate Ryder awoke so slowly that early June morning that her happy dream of her brother stayed with her through the soft clucking of the hens and the sharp splash of water being pumped into a pail in the farmyard below. Ralph, she thought sleepily, was washing his grinning, freckled face and smoothing down his rumpled hair. In a moment he would turn around and shout up to her to come down and join him.

And then she opened her eyes to the paling night—and remembered it all.

Ralph had gone off to sea. He had left them.

A great dreariness crept up over her from the shadowy corners of the bedroom, causing her such misery that she lay without moving in the big bed, praying that the pain would leave her before Priscilla, lying beside her, awoke and thrust herself upon the day. In her anguish she saw her life here at High Ashfield, now that Ralph was gone, more blackly than she had ever seen it before.

The horrible war was never going to end. She and

her mother and Adam and Priscilla would have to go on toiling to save the farm to the end of time.

When Ralph had been at home, the two of them had laughed at their troubles and had gone rolling down Wash Meadow hill, over and over—now green grass, now blue sky—right down to the river's edge, forgetting the day's hard words in the joy of each other. But now that he had left, she had to face the truth alone: four years their father had been away from them all—four long years, fighting against King Charles—and the grinding drudgery of working his land was *destroying* them all.

Her mother, whom she loved, was growing sharper-tongued with every weary month; Adam was becoming more silent and withdrawn; and Priscilla, daily crosser and more difficult to live with. As for herself, she was hardly better than her sister. She knew that she was often moody and lazy and bored. In the last sad weeks, trying to shut out the grief of Ralph's going, she had lost herself in dreams of her father, whom she could not remember, or else stolen away to the apple loft with one of his precious books, and forgotten to feed the hens.

She lay on, still without moving, thinking of the tedious, leaden day that lay ahead, praying hard that someone or something would make her laugh again.

Everything was bearable, if only one could laugh.

Searching for laughter, she came upon Tamsin. Tamsin Pascoe. Her friend from Langby. And, thinking of Tamsin, she turned over in bed and lay on her back, stretching her feet down between the harsh, hempen sheets, smiling inwardly at the warmth of Tamsin's fun.

But it was only for a moment.

Feeling the coldness and emptiness beside her with her feet, she shot wide awake and sat up. Priscilla was up already! She stared unbelievingly at her empty half of the bed. For the first time in her life, her elder sister had got up and dressed and gone down to the milking without kicking her out of bed first.

The Lord be praised for His wonders, she thought, eying the hollow left in the bolster by Priscilla's head.

Then, pulling the sheet back close up around her shoulders, she settled back, smiling, and returned to her thoughts of Tamsin.

Five minutes later she was roused by her mother's voice.

"Kate," her mother shouted up the stairs. "None of your lolloping in bed, child. Get up quickly. You'll have to help them at the clipping."

Help them at the clipping? She jumped out of bed, hardly believing her ears. She had never done such a thing before in her life. Neither had Priscilla. She pulled on her shift in a hurry before her luck changed.

"Wear your torn dress."

"Yes, Mother," she shouted down to her. "Yes, I will."

Standing up in the half darkness struggling into her old clothes, she felt the gloom of her waking rolling away like morning mist when the sun comes out. No hoeing of peas today. No weeding of marjoram and mint. No carding of greasy wool. She was going to do something quite new. She was going to help Adam and old Smy as they sheared the sheep.

"But that's *boy's* work, Mother," she heard Priscilla protesting in the kitchen below.

Her voice came up shrilly through the cracks in the boards.

"With Ralph gone," came her mother's tart retort, "we haven't got a boy."

The bleakness of this truth hit Kate in the midriff, and she tugged on her dress so fiercely that she ripped the tear in the hem wider still.

3

"But you can't send her out with the men. It's not . . . it's not fitting."

"Fitting? Fiddlesticks," her mother slapped out. "She's still a child. She's not learned yet to finnick and give herself airs."

"She's *not* a child. She's twelve years old."

Kate caught her breath. She could not bear the thought of Priscilla spoiling her bright day; so she ran downstairs barefoot—and only half-dressed—to stop her sister from doing any more harm.

But it only made matters worse.

"*Look* at her, Mother!" Priscilla exclaimed, suddenly bursting into tears. "She's . . . she's a yeoman's daughter. Not . . . not a beggar's."

Her mother looked up angrily from cutting the men's midday cheese and frowned at Kate's disheveled appearance.

"Wash your face at the pump, child," she ordered sharply, "and then comb the tangles out of your hair."

Once out in the farmyard, Kate dipped her hands in the leathern bucket by the pump and then gazed through the wetness at the familiar world of outdoors. In the cool, dawning light the dung heap was smoking softly. Around its base the hens were pecking for maggots and worms. Old Steadfast, her father's lame cavalry horse, on holiday from the plow, stood with his head over the half door of the stable staring at her, too lazy even to blink. She wiped her face on the sleeve of her dress and ran her fingers hopefully through her hair and then stood for a moment, breathing in the tranquil rightness of all that she saw: the clean barn, the new patch in the reed thatch, the walnut tree, the mended gate, the paling eastern sky. This was her home, her world. For all the drudgery and the cross words, for all her loneliness now that Ralph was gone, she loved it. She loved everything about it.

4

Faintly, from two fields away, she could hear the lambs, separated from the ewes, bleating in the fold.

She ran back into the house, longing to have breakfast behind her and to be out with Adam and old Smy under the clipping tree, and found her mother in the kitchen alone.

"Eat it up quickly," she said, putting a bowl of hot porridge on the table. "With you to handle the ewes and to fold the fleeces, the two of them'll save a morning . . . maybe a whole day."

A clash of pails along the flagged passage and a hiccuping sob told her that Priscilla had taken her grief to the dairy.

Her mother went over to the low kitchen window and stooped down to peer up at the sky.

"The Lord willing, it'll stay fine," she announced, straightening her back and reaching for the earthenware jug of small ale to fill up the men's bottles.

It was about time the Lord did a little willing, Kate thought irreverently between hot mouthfuls. Ever since Ralph had left home, the Almighty had neglected them sadly at High Ashfield. He had allowed it to rain all April and the first half of May and had done nothing to stop the cleavers choking up the winter corn, so that what with the bad weather and their having to rake the clingers out of the wheat, Adam and Smy were weeks behind with the work of the farm. The fallow was not dunged nor the thistles and fitches weeded out of the barley. And if June turned hot—as Bet Smy's aching knees predicted it would—then the High Meadow would be ripe for mowing before the middle of the month. And before they all went mowing on top of the hill, she thought wearily as she scraped the bottom of the bowl, she and Priscilla had to wash the new wool and pull the stinkweed out of the flax . . . and the bees would be swarming . . .

5

"Kate," said her mother quietly with her back still turned to her. "Kate . . . you'll be a yeoman's daughter again . . . when your father comes home . . . when the war's over."

She looked at her mother's tired back and listened to the quiet voice and felt obscurely hurt. First Priscilla. Now her mother . . .

"It can't be long, child. The King must surrender soon."

But Kate had no thought for King Charles. The hurt inside her had grown to a pain.

"But I'm a yeoman's daughter *now*, Mother," she blurted out. "Don't you think I am?"

Her mother turned with the beginnings of a smile in her eyes. Then, looking down at her still seated at the table, she frowned instead.

"Not with that head of hair, you aren't," she snapped angrily. "I told you to comb it, Kate. Go and do so at once."

She stumbled up the stairs, bewildered that a few tangles should call down such wrath.

"The Lord can forgive poverty, child, and a homely face," her mother shouted up after her. "But never the slovenliness of a slut."

A homely face?

So she was ugly as well as everything else, she thought somberly as she walked up the lane with her heavy basket toward the bleating sheep. Well, her ugliness was the Lord's fault, not her own. Somehow— and sometime—she would have to learn to forgive Him for His mistake.

Yet, she could hardly feel churlish with Him just now. Not today. For the sun had climbed out of the low mist that shrouded the North Sea, and the bramble fronds in the hedges and the grass at her feet were sparkling with drops of light. She heard again the cry of

6

the sheep, and she felt excited. The task that lay ahead of her made her feel wanted and in some way important.

She came at last to the gate and saw Adam and the old hired man a long way off, setting hurdles for the clipping pen under the great oak tree. Adam looked distracted. He was moving three hurdles to Smy's one and then standing stock still, gazing toward the village, lost in thought. She sighed. Her brother was unhappy again. And when he was unhappy, he shouted at fools.

But it proved not too difficult, this job of Ralph's.

She had to bring the sheep to the shearers and then let them out into the field through the gate in the fold when they had been shorn. In between times she had to fold the new-fallen fleeces inside out and then from side to side, tie them with the draggled wool of the tail, and throw them on the heap with the others.

Surely, if she kept her wits about her, she could not go wrong?

Most of the ewes were as meek and resigned as almshouse women, and she was able to lead rather than drag them to the shearing tools. But then came a ram, who dug his sharp feet into the turf, stiffened the muscles at the back of his legs, and refused to budge.

"Grasp him by the horns, Kate," Adam shouted. "You can tug as hard as you like. They won't come off in your hands."

Smy grinned toothlessly and nodded his head in agreement.

So tug she did, pitting her whole strength against the stubborn beast. The ram bared his teeth at her wickedly, struggled, lowered his head as though to butt, thought better of it, struggled again—and at last gave in.

Boy's work, indeed!

At midday, when the long shadow of the clipping tree had shrunk to a round pool beneath their feet, Adam called a halt.

"No, not another ewe, Kate," he called out over the buzzing of the flies. "I'm hungry. Where've you put the basket?"

"How am I doing?" she asked shyly as they walked together toward the food.

"Fine."

"As good as Ralph?"

"Couldn't tell the difference. Except that brother Ralph wouldn't have trailed a great hank of skirt in all that sheep muck."

8

And smiling, he stooped down and ripped off her loose hem.

He sent her up to the High Meadow with her hunk of bread and cheese and told her to sleep if she wanted to.

"I'll wake you when we want you," he called after her.

But she did not sleep. She was too excited by the unusualness of the day and too thankful and relieved that Adam was pleased with her.

She sat, instead, by the gate into the High Meadow on the edge of the tall grass and looked down the slope beyond the crying lambs and the shorn sheep and the two shearers, dozing under the clipping tree, to the farmhouse and—beyond the farmhouse—to the valley where the River Colne, shrunk to the width of a great ditch, wound its way northward to Colchester between glistening stretches of wet mud. There was not a sail to be seen anywhere on its water, not even an oyster boat or a punt. High in the sky, a solitary sea gull was flying in from the sea. Below, the river world slumbered and waited for the flood of the incoming tide and for the wherries and smacks, brigantines, and hoys outward bound from Colchester or sailing up from the coast.

She gazed at the shrunken river and longed for Friday's high tide, for it would bring Uncle Ben's *Essex Maid* and his youngest apprentice seaman, her brother Ralph, not home to them, it is true, but at least sailing past at the bottom of their meadows as the hoy made for port at the Hythe. Uncle Ben did good business carrying bags of hops, sacks of wheat, cheeses, apples, and the weavers' bales of coarse woolen Colchester cloth from the little port southward down the coast and up the Thames to Smart's Quay near Billingsgate in the City of London, returning within the week to Essex with a cargo of manufactured goods. So that, come Friday, Kate was all eyes for the familiar sail in the river; and when she saw it—and her mother's back was turned—she ran pell-mell to their jetty to wave to Ralph as the ship glided by.

"Old Sally's farrowed," she would shout.

"How many?"

"Ten. But the runt's died. How's London?"

"Smoky and stinking," he would shout back. "Always is. There's been a riot."

"What about? Where?"

" 'Prentice boys," his voice would float back to her from away upstream. "Smithfield Market."

The *Essex Maid* spent twenty-four hours at the Hythe, unloading her cargo and taking on a new consignment of cloth and country produce, and then slipped down the river on the strong ebb tide so swiftly that, like as not, Kate missed her passing.

Kate sat that sunny June midday with the bees buzzing in the clover behind her, turning her gaze idly toward Adam, stirring beneath the clipping tree and now standing up and stretching himself.

Now, he stood quite still, staring—as she had stared—at the shrunken river and the glistening mud.

Looking at him, her heart missed a beat. Seen from behind, there was an air of utter hopelessness in his stance.

This was not unhappiness. It was despair. The despair was so strong that it came wafting over the pasture and up to the hill where she sat.

Adam was seventeen. He was a man. She sat there, watching him, completely bewildered by his grown-up grief.

All afternoon Kate tugged at the ewes and struggled with the rams and folded the fleeces, while the sun poured down and the lambs cried and the flies buzzed about her head. She felt dazed by the heat and the monotony of it all.

It's now that I'm going to do something stupid, she

thought, sensing that she was almost asleep on her feet.

And then, she suddenly saw it! Gazing drowsily up the hill while waiting for Smy to finish his ewe, she saw a familiar tall, black hat bobbing up and down on the far side of the hedge.

It was Parson Pratt, afar off, trotting down the lane to the farm to visit her mother.

Adam must have seen the hat, too.

"Go and see what the old fool wants," he threw at her over his shoulder.

Wide awake in the instant, she ran off to beat the parson to the gate, astonishment and laughter catching at her throat. She could hardly believe it. Adam had called him "an old fool." *Adam!* Not Ralph.

She scrambled over the gate and stood in the middle of the way, waiting for the minister to appear around the last corner in the lane. Was it great news that he brought? News of victory? Of the King's final surrender? Or bad news? Of a Parliament defeat? Or just middling, everyday news: of swine fever or a new tax—or God's special favor to Mr. Pratt? God was always showering homely blessings upon Mr. Pratt; and Mr. Pratt was always trotting down the lane from the village to tell their mother all about them.

As she stood waiting, trying to quiet her breath, a huge hope dawned in her mind. What with the West Country subdued and the King fled to the north and Oxford surrounded, it must be news of the signing of the peace that brought Mr. Pratt down their lane. Victory at last!

She thought of her father and crossed her fingers and prayed that it was so.

The lean old man on his lean horse appeared almost at once, and her happiness plummeted down to the depths. The parson was sitting hunched up in his saddle and his face was grim.

"Woe unto Jerusalem," he said, reining in his nag. "And woe, woe upon us for our sins."

"What's happened, Mr. Pratt?" she asked, sick at heart.

"Once more, once more, my child, the Lord's enemies have risen against us. From all sides they come about us."

Charles Stuart and the Scots had come to terms and an Irish army was about to join them. They had heard the news in the House of Commons not two days back.

"So . . . so the war's not over? Not over at all?"

The old man shook his head.

"All's to do again, Katherine," he said brokenly, as he picked up his reins.

"And Father won't come home?"

No. Their father would not come home.

"Pray to God to forgive us our unworthiness, my child. Pray to God!"

She looked sadly at his stooped shoulders as he went down the lane.

"Yes, I will, Mr. Pratt," she whispered after him.

Back under the clipping tree, the ram Smy was shearing was crying so loudly that Kate had to shout when she told Adam the bad tidings.

"It's all rumor," Adam shouted back, as he hauled another ewe across his knees. "The Irish haven't landed, have they? The Scots haven't marched south?"

"No, but Charles Stuart has made a pact with them," she replied, as she stopped to fold a fleece. "They said so in the House of Commons."

Adam threw the ewe out of his lap, got up, and strode toward her.

"You said *what?*" he shouted, his eyes blazing.

"Charles Stuart," she repeated, bewildered by his anger. "Charles Stuart's made a pact . . ."

The next moment he was shaking her fiercely by the shoulders.

"He's your King, Kate. Your *King!*" he stormed.

She looked up at him, appalled.

"Never again let me hear you call him anything but your King."

"But . . . but that's . . . that's what Mr. Pratt called him," she stammered, the tears shooting up into her eyes. "I . . . I only told you what he said."

"To hell with Mr. Pratt," he shouted. "Father hasn't been fighting all these years to turn the King off his throne. He's been fighting to uphold our English law. You know that, Kate, as well as I do."

And he strode back to his stool and hauled the ewe savagely back onto his knees.

She was not only frightened but horribly confused. She could not think why he was so angry with her. She had always thought that King Charles was her father's greatest enemy.

Blinded by her tears, she stooped to grope for the fleece she had been folding, tripped over it, and fell into the mire.

"You'd better go home," Adam said roughly, as she picked herself up. "You've done enough."

"There's still more fleeces to fold," she replied stubbornly.

"Leave'n be, mawther, I'll do 'n," rumbled old Smy.

But with the flies now settling on the sheep droppings fouling her clothes, she stood her ground, tossing aside the folded fleece and stooping for another.

"I said go home," whipped out Adam. "Do as you're told."

She straightened up, scowled, and flung away from the clipping tree, bitterly unhappy and angry with her brother. He had been unkind. Unjust.

Hidden from him, at length, by the high hedge, she

stopped in her running and gazed over a gate down into the valley at the tide flooding in. Two wherries were sailing up to the Hythe. At sight of them she burst out crying.

She could not understand at all why the bright day had fallen about her in ruins.

The High Meadow

2

Next morning, the sun beat down on the farmstead. Blackbirds whistled; bees buzzed; butterflies basked against the garden wall. And Adam and Smy, the shearing finished, began dunging the fallow.

As she hoed the peas, Kate watched her brother passing and repassing her with his steaming load, hoping for something—she knew not what. A word, perhaps. Or a smile. Something to explain to her the true meaning of what had happened under the clipping tree. But he plodded past each time, his face shut away against intrusion. And so it went on all that sunlit week. Adam went about his work, not so much avoiding her as failing to have her in his thoughts.

Later, they all trooped up to Langby to help Mrs. Cooper and Tamsin and Simon mow their hay; and in the fun and laughter of the mowing, her hurt and bewilderment slowly faded from her mind. What she had said about the King remained as one of those inexplicably dreadful things that one did when one was young. Adam's frightening anger was best forgotten.

And then, on that Saturday, came the letter from Uncle Ben.

She could think of nothing but the joy that it brought. Ralph was to come back to them for two whole days.

Uncle Ben wrote that the High Meadow must be nearly ripe for mowing and that could Adam and the grass but wait till next Friday, when the hoy would come again to the Hythe, then he would send Ralph up to them to help with the hay.

On that last Friday in June, Ralph walked up from the towpath through the dusk, swinging his seaman's bundle and whistling a new tune.

"Ralph, Ralph," she shouted.

She ran in the direction of the Wash Meadow gate and was in time to see him vaulting nimbly over it and striding on toward her, a small, dark, jaunty figure against the western sky.

"Kate, ahoy!" he cried, throwing his bundle up in the air. "Here I am, home again!"

She hugged him so tightly—in such a fever of happiness—that he was startled.

"What's the matter?" he asked.

"Nothing," she replied, laughing. "Except you're home."

"And the High Meadow? We're going to mow it tomorrow?"

She nodded.

"Simon and Tamsin are coming over with the Coopers' hired man."

Ralph sighed with relief. He had been so afraid, he said, that they might have finished the hay harvest before he got back.

"No," she explained. "We mowed the Coopers' hay first. We all went to Langby last week."

Next morning she had her heart's desire. She was

standing behind Ralph on the edge of High Meadow, trying not to laugh.

"Ralph's a poor hand with a scythe," Adam had told his mother.

Yet "poor" was not the right word. "Original" or "seaman-like" was better. He jabbed at the grass in short, sharp strokes—as one would row a boat in a high sea—sending dodder grass and moon daisies flying through the air. She had to collect the wrack with her hay rake from a wide circle and sometimes even had to pull it out of their hair with her hands.

"I'll get the hang of it in time," he said cheerfully as he pulled the tip of the scythe out of the ground for the third time in three minutes. "Then we'll overhaul the others. You see if we don't."

But Kate liked things as they were. Smy and old Bet and Mrs. Cooper's hired man and his wife were mowing on the far side of the meadow. With the measured swings of the scythe that are perfected by a lifetime of mowing, the old men had cut two long swaths right along by the hedge, while in the middle of the meadow, Adam and Priscilla and Tamsin and her brother, Simon, were mowing fitfully between bursts of laughter. Left far behind, islanded by the grass, Kate had her brother to herself.

There was so much that she wanted to ask him— privately—just between the two of them.

"Do you *really* like it?" she began shyly as she raked in the mown grass. "Like it at sea?"

"It's a man's life," he replied grandly, tossing a clump of buttercups high in the air.

Then he stopped mowing, turned toward her, and added more frankly, "Well, I couldn't go on staying here."

"Why not?" she asked, astonished.

He stared at her in wonder.

"But, Kate, it's *Father's* farm."

"I know it is."

"And if Father gets killed, it goes to Adam. And if Adam dies, then it goes to his children. High Ashfield will never, never be mine."

She must have known this dimly, but she had not understood what it meant.

"So . . . so you don't really like it . . . at all?" she asked, feeling a lump in her throat.

She could not bear Ralph not to be happy.

"Of course I do," he grinned.

Life on the hoy, he said, was much more hardwork-
ing than he had ever thought it would be. And at times it
was plain boring. But he liked the sea. Liked feeling that
he was going somewhere—even though the somewhere
was only Smart's Quay with its porters and doxies and
piles of lading. Anyhow, it was *his* life. And he was
learning a trade.

"And Uncle Ben?"

Ralph smiled ruefully.

"He's a powerful hand with a rope end!"

"He beats you?"

"Of course he beats me. But he's just. And . . .
and . . ."

Kate looked up at him quickly and saw an expression on his face which she knew of old. Ralph wanted to
tell her something. Something secret. Something that
ought not to be told.

"Knight's honor?" he said. "On Excalibur?"

"Knight's honor," she replied.

"He says that . . . if I learn my trade . . . and don't
fall overboard and get drowned. And . . . and if he
doesn't marry one of his doxies and . . . and get children
. . . then he'll leave me the hoy in his will."

Her mind was in a whirl. She did not understand
about doxies and did not like to ask. But it seemed good
news—good news for Ralph—out of this man's world.

"You don't ever fall overboard, do you?" she asked
anxiously.

"I did once . . . in the first week. The boom
knocked me off my feet . . . going down the river."

He turned back to his hacking of the grass; and she, left to her raking, thought how little she knew about Adam, Ralph, anybody. She had known Ralph, she had thought, as she had known herself. Yet she had never guessed that he had left home because he must—not because he wanted to.

"Where's the lunch, Kate?" he asked after a few minutes.

"You're not hungry already?"

"Of course I am. I'm always hungry."

The food and the small beer were buried deep in the long grass in the shade of a crab-apple tree by the hedge.

As she watched his white teeth tearing into one of Priscilla's meat pasties, all that was twisted and tangled inside her seemed to smooth out. She might not have understood him, but he was just the same. He had weathered a little; his freckles were darker and his eyebrows were bleached. But he was the old Ralph. Not a new one. He was as solid and unchangeable as the walnut tree.

She would tell him her trouble.

"Knight's honor?" she began.

"Knight's honor," he replied, looking up in surprise, in the middle of a mouthful.

"Adam's got something on his mind. He's unhappy."

A fresh burst of laughter drew their eyes to a group in the middle of the meadow. Tamsin was crowning Adam's head with a ring of moon daisies.

"Doesn't look as though he's unhappy," Ralph said with a grin.

"That's because you're here . . . and the Pascoes."

She told him then of the day that she had helped Adam at the shearing and of his terrible anger with her for repeating what Mr. Pratt had called the King.

"Was it a very dreadful thing to have called him?" she asked.

Ralph frowned, deep in thought, as puzzled as herself.

"I don't know," he said at last.

There was much talk in London against the King, he went on. Armies of Parliament had defeated him in the field. That was certain. But the King refused to end the bloodshed by coming to terms.

"And now he's trying to get the Scots and the Irish and the French to fight against us," he said with a burst of indignation. "Against *us*, Kate—his Englishmen."

"So some people hate him?"

"A great many."

"And they want to push him off his throne?"

"I don't know. They might."

Kate thought about this, chewing hard on a grass stem.

"Does Uncle Ben ever call the King 'Charles Stuart'?" she asked.

Ralph laughed. It was a great, noisy "Ralph" laugh. Uncle Ben called the King much worse names than the name he was born with, he said.

Then he added, more seriously, "But he says King Charles is the King of England. He's the only king we've got. Now we've defeated him, he'll just *have* to submit to ruling us with a parliament."

"And if he won't?"

Ralph's brow puckered up.

"I don't know what'll happen, Kate. I really don't."

Kate gazed unseeing across the pleasant meadow, still burdened by her trouble. Uncle Ben seemed to think about the King much as Adam did—though not with such passion. That was good. That was a relief. But what about the soldiers who had fought the war? What about their father? "Father hasn't been fighting all these years to turn the King off his throne," Adam had said. But how did he know? Adam had not stood beside him at

Edgehill, at Marston Moor, at Naseby. Adam had not seen his best friends killed.

"Do you think Father calls the King 'Charles Stuart'?" she blurted out.

Ralph turned to her quickly.

"Father?"

Then he looked away over the swaying grass, frowning with perplexity.

Neither of them knew what their father thought about King Charles. How could they? They had only seen him once in the last four years, and then only briefly when he had ridden down into Essex to secure fresh mounts. He was a stranger to them. A legend. To Kate he was little more than a kindly presence who had lifted her up on his knee and taught her to read. Ralph, being two years older, remembered more.

"Surely you remember his first going, Kate?" he had asked her over and over again. "Father and his friends . . . they rode out of High Ashfield singing. They stopped and plucked roses out of the hedge."

But Kate had always shaken her head. She had not remembered. And in the years that had followed, ashamed of her forgetting, she had put a bright sword into his hand and mounted him on a black charger and sent him galloping off out of Essex, drums beating and a trumpet blowing, his silken scarf streaming in the wind. Such a father deserved nothing less.

"I don't know what Father calls the King," said Ralph at last.

All that both of them knew was that, unlike Uncle Ben, he had fought a most terrible war. In battle, he had always been posted in the most dangerous stations—far ahead of the main army—in the outposts. This last winter, at the siege of Exeter, he had been watching with his regiment every night, cold and exposed and always in peril. Their mother had worried greatly about him in that western campaign. The war seemed never-ending, she had grieved, and he was growing old. When he wrote to her, he did not complain. He did not tell her in bitterness what he thought of the King. He wrote, instead, about the men from the neighborhood of High Ashfield who were under his command. Would she send to Wivenhoe, he directed, and tell Timothy Ling's wife that he was healed of his wound. Would she send comforts to the Howletts; their father had been killed. He sent instructions, too, about the farm. Adam must sow oats this year in the thirty-acre field. He must look to the thatch on the barn.

Ralph's thoughts must have come back to the present. He jumped to his feet, wiped his mouth with his sleeve, and held out both hands to pull Kate up.

"It's time we got back to the mowing," he said.

Their poor little patch of hacked meadow was a reproach to them. The two laborers and their wives had reached the far hedge some time ago and had turned and were coming back, their scythes swinging evenly like the pendulums of clocks. They had almost reached the group still fooling about in the middle of the meadow. They must all hurry, Kate thought. It was the Lord's day tomorrow. They must finish the mowing tonight.

"Don't worry about Father," Ralph tossed back over his shoulder with his first flurry of flying grass. "He'll soon be home to tell us himself what he thinks of the King. It can't be long."

And because Ralph was as dependable as the walnut tree—and because more than three-quarters of the High Meadow had still to be mowed—her trouble took itself off to the back of her mind.

They hacked and raked, hacked and raked, each glad of the other, each glad of the sun and the hissing of the scythe and the heady smell of the mown grass.

Ten minutes later a fresh burst of laughter came

from the middle of the meadow. They looked up. It was Priscilla this time who had made a ring of flowers. She was crowning Simon Pascoe.

Kate scowled.

"I wish they'd stop being so foolish," she said severely, "and let Adam and Simon get on."

Ralph laughed.

"It'll be your turn in another few years," he threw back at her.

"What do you mean?"

"They're practicing trying to get themselves husbands, of course."

"Ralph," she exclaimed, amazed, grabbing at his arm so that he had to stop mowing. "What are you saying?"

Ralph grinned at her.

"But it's obvious."

"Priscilla? Tamsin? Getting husbands?"

"All girls are like that," he told her sagely.

Smart's Quay seemed to have taught him a great deal.

"But Priscilla . . ." she began, still astonished. And then she thought: well, Priscilla was sixteen, she was not happy with her mother, she must get a husband sometime. But . . . so soon! And Simon . . . Simon Pascoe! Kate did not like Tamsin's brother; she thought him vain and foolish—and dishonest.

"But not *Tamsin*, Ralph," she burst out, even more shocked.

Tamsin was less than three years older than herself. She was barely fifteen. Tamsin belonged to *her* world— not to Adam's.

"Oh, don't be so serious, Kate," he said, laughing at her expression. "They're only having fun."

She went back to her raking, feeling sullen. She did not like Tamsin to be having that sort of fun—not with Adam. Tamsin was *her* friend. They exchanged riddles and jokes and sang songs together. Besides, Tamsin would not suit Adam for the length of an afternoon; she was far too generous and unthinking and gay. Kate dug savagely at a clump of ladies' smock. She felt sullen, too, about herself. She had been a fool; she had lived with her eyes shut. And now that they were open she felt like a startled donkey, not knowing which way to look first.

And then she heard Tamsin's voice coming to her over the grass.

"Kate, Kate," Tamsin shouted, laughing. "Look at our two June kings! Hurry up and make Ralph a crown . . . and then we'll have three."

The sun swooped back into the sky.

"Yes . . . yes, I will," Kate shouted back, swept again for the moment with joy. "I'll make it of buttercups . . . so his face'll be all yellow."

A golden Ralph, the pollen dusting his freckles. That was it.

It was Ralph who saw their mother first. He had stopped to sharpen his scythe and had turned back toward Kate to show her proudly how he did it. He saw her over Kate's shoulder.

"There's Mother!" he exclaimed. "Surely it's not noon?"

Kate turned to look, too.

Their mother made a kind of festival of the hay harvest, especially when it was the High Meadow that was being mown. For the meadow was *hers;* she had brought it to their father in her dowry. Today, she was to leave her work and bring the first strawberries and to stay and eat with them.

Kate frowned as she watched her struggling up the lane.

"There's something wrong," she said.

Her mother was walking in too much haste.

"Ralph. Kate," she called up to them.

Her voice had an oddly strangled, young sort of sound for their mother.

They dropped their tools and ran to her.

She had stopped in the middle of the lane and was getting her breath.

"Ben's sent word . . . your father . . . he's ill . . . very ill. I must go to him."

Standing there, she looked strangely defenseless.

"Mother, sit down," said Ralph. "I'll get the others."

Kate sat by her side on the hedge bank, moved beyond tears by her plight.

"It's a camp fever, Kate," she said brokenly.

Their father was lying in a farmhouse north of Oxford, she told them when they all came up. It would take too long to go by sea . . . so Uncle Ben was hiring her a seat in one of Mr. Wigmore's great wagons.

"Either you or Ralph must drive me into Colchester," she said to Adam.

"But, Mother . . ." broke in Priscilla, "it . . . it's the Lord's day tomorrow."

Their mother got to her feet. That was why they must hurry, she replied. Mr. Wigmore's wagon of Colchester cloth left the town soon after two. She would be in Chelmsford before seven and safe at her sister's at Boyton Cross before dusk.

"Come Monday, your Uncle Seth'll find me carriage farther west."

It was Ralph and Kate who drove her into town.

Kate sat in the back of the cart facing backward, clutching her mother's hasty bundle, much shaken by the news of her father's danger and by the glimpse she had caught into her mother's heart. Her mother had always seemed so strong, so certain, so unflinching a bulwark in all their childhood griefs that Kate, in her childishness, had overlooked that her mother had been a woman and their father's wife before ever she had been their mother. And then she thought how cruelly things had worked out. Uncle Ben had sent word that Oxford had fallen at last. The long war must be over. And yet their father might well be dying. After all these years—just at the end—he might die of camp fever in a distant farm and never come home to them all at High Ashfield.

When they came to the Harwich road and rattled over East Bridge, she turned around in the cart and gazed at the great walls of the ancient citadel. They clattered through the East Gate and slowly lumbered up the steep incline of East Hill.

"Your uncle said that he would wait for us in King Street," said their mother.

"There he is!" exclaimed Ralph, giving old Steadfast a flick with the whip. "There's Uncle Ben."

"Where?"

"West-northwest. No. Not that way. To starboard."

"Outside St. Runwald's Church, Mother," said Kate gently.

Waiting

3

The first things that Kate saw when the two of them got back to the High Meadow late that afternoon were the three crowns of the June kings thrown down on the hedge bank by the gate; the moon daisies and sorrel had wilted in the heat. Beyond them, at the far end of the meadow, the four mowers were working grimly and in silence.

Tamsin, seeing their return, slipped away from her task and ran to meet them.

"Your mother?" she asked simply. "You saw her to the wagon?"

Kate nodded. And her friend, touching her gently on the arm, ran back to her brother without a single useless word.

"We've still got hours of work if we're to finish tonight," said Ralph, picking up his scythe and slashing down his first swath.

And Kate, sad of heart—but oddly grateful for Tamsin's touch—picked up her rake and combed out the bundle of grass.

On and on the ten of them worked till dusk fell and

the birds stopped singing. And still they mowed—the swinging of scythes and the dragging of the rakes racking their bodies but dulling the pain in their hearts. A moon came up behind the trees, and Kate, leaning wearily on the handle of her rake, watched Smy cut the last swath in a silver glimmer that blanched his face and turned the buttercups white.

Then the two families bade one another a good night, soberly and quietly as befitted friends in a common trouble. Then took their several ways: Simon and Tamsin and their aunt's servants up the hill to Langby, the Smys across the fields to their cottage, and Kate and Priscilla and their two brothers down the lane to the empty farmhouse.

It was a comfortless homecoming. No light, no fire, no hot food, no mother were awaiting them.

"I'm too weary to read aloud from the Bible," said Adam, when they had eaten again of bread and cheese. "Let us each say our prayers to ourselves . . . and go to bed."

Next morning Kate awoke to find sunlight pouring in through the bedroom window and Priscilla still asleep at her side. She sat up in panic. Something terrible must have happened. She had never woken to sunlight—broad sunlight—before.

And then she remembered.

A smell of frying coming up through the floorboards and a cautious moving about in the kitchen below told her that, though she and her sister were still abed, at least someone was up.

She slipped out of bed and crept down the stairs and found Ralph.

"Goodness!" she exclaimed, seeing what he was doing.

He had pulled down the largest pan from its hook and was frying not one egg or two . . . but about ten.

"I've never seen such a lot of fried eggs," she burst out.

"I'm hungry," he muttered. "Don't wake the others."

"Mother only allows us one as a treat," she whispered.

Ralph knew this as well as she.

"A man must eat," he whispered, unrepentant, shaking the pan. "I don't mind giving you two."

And so it went on all day. It was a holiday from their mother, but a horrible holiday, remembering its cause.

After breakfast she wandered into the house room and stared gloomily at her mother's chair and her spindle and loom and then at the painted cloth of Naomi and Ruth hanging on the wall, which her mother had brought with her to High Ashfield on her marriage. In the last few months Kate had longed so often to be out of range of her mother's sharp tongue—just for a day, just for an hour—that each kindly remembrance of her now gave her a stab of remorse. She escaped into the parlor to console herself by fingering the fine coverlid that hung on the best bed. It was forbidden for any of them to touch this coverlid that their grandmother had made; but the feel of its exquisite stitchery impelled her. It was as necessary to stroke it as it was to stroke a rose petal or the bloom on a plum. Then she looked up and caught sight of her father's few books high on their shelf and the empty hooks in the wall where his musket had hung before the war—and she fled.

Everything everywhere spoke to her of her parents.

She found Ralph outside in the garden at the front of the house, looking as disconsolate as she felt. He was frowning up at the Tudor roses incised in the cracking pargeting.

"The whole house wants new plaster," he muttered. ". . . If only anybody's got the time."

She and Ralph felt the same way about their home. They loved it. That morning their eyes turned together to their grandfather's proud boast to the world carved in crude letters on the great overhanging crossbeam—TOM RYDER MADE THIS HOUSE. 1599—and then traveled along the beam to where Grandfather Tom had carved a rustic St. George killing his dragon. The dragon's tongue shot around the corner of the house and pointed its tip at the beehives standing in the orchard. Far back in their childhood their father had touched up the whole carving in bright colors so that the tongue had looked like a scarlet lick coming around the corner. But now, tongue and dragon and knight were all weather-beaten and faded.

As he gazed at the carving, Ralph visibly brightened.

"Kate," he said. "I'd love to paint it up again. Do you think God would mind me painting it on the sabbath?"

She shook her head. She felt doubtful less about God than about Priscilla. Priscilla thought both the boast and the carving were vulgar. The Ryders had come up in the world since Grandfather's day.

"Better not," she said, sorely tempted as she gazed at the faded St. George. "Priscilla'll say you've broken the fourth commandment."

Adam was angry with them both for not having woken him earlier; and, an hour later, behind with the milking and the feeding of the stock, all four of them walked up to the church in a temper.

"You're a fool, Ralph. And Kate, you're no better," Adam flared at them. "You heard the cows lowing . . ."

"You and Priscilla . . ." Ralph swung back at him. "You shouldn't have lain hoggishly in bed."

"Hoggishly?" gasped Priscilla—and took the affront out on Kate.

Her appearance was disgraceful, Priscilla snapped. She was ashamed to take her into church with her.

"Put straight your bodice. Pull up your hose."

At which Kate scowled and sulked, refusing to do either.

What a hateful family we are! she thought, as they filed up the churchyard path. Pray God, Mr. Pratt and his sermon will bring us back to grace.

Both failed. The sermon dealt with the sins of Sodom and Gomorrah; and Mr. Pratt was more zealous in saving souls than he was in ministering to poor broken human hearts.

"Katherine, my dear child," he said, when he spoke to them after the service, "our prayers to the Lord have been answered."

"Answered?" Kate blurted out in amazement.

"Oxford has fallen. The Lord's enemies are confounded."

"You . . . you haven't heard about Father?"

He bowed his head. Yes, he had heard of their grief, he said. And he sorrowed for them. He sorrowed for them deeply.

"But, ah, my children," he said, turning to the others, "you must bear your cross with gladness. The Lord loves those whom He chastises. He has singled you out for His love."

"By making Father ill?" burst out Ralph.

"By sending you this trial, my son."

"Like when He sent a bee to sting you on the nose?" Ralph snorted, scarlet with anger.

Adam pulled him away quickly and dragged him down the lane.

"You fool!" he hissed.

But he said no more. None of them said any more. It was a most wretched day.

Priscilla burned the bacon that they were to have eaten for their dinner; and not one of them had a heart

for the strawberry tarts that their mother had baked in Ralph's honor. As for Ralph himself, he was so angry with Mr. Pratt and so bitterly unhappy that he flung himself out of the kitchen soon after their return, telling them all that he wanted to be alone.

To comfort herself in so much sadness, Kate stole one of her father's volumes of Hakluyt's *Voyages* out of the parlor and read it in the High Meadow. It was a thing forbidden for her to take one of his precious books out into the fields, but she felt, somehow, that could her father but know her straits, he would forgive her disobedience. Why should he have taught her how to read and put her in the way of so much comfort and joy if she were not to use them in her distress? His little library had opened for her a secret world of men's courage and hopes and high endeavor, a world unknown—or else unheeded—by everyone at High Ashfield save her brother Ralph. The two of them had sailed with Sir

Francis Drake up the western coast of New Spain. They had traveled overland with Job Hortop and seen crocodiles and oysters growing on trees. They had known the terrors of the Inquisition. And when Hakluyt was done, they had taken to Malory's *Morte d'Arthur* and fought side by side with King Arthur's knights.

Ralph found her out as the hedge shadows were lengthening across the mown grass.

"Here you are!" he exclaimed. "I've been looking for you everywhere."

Then, seeing what she was at, he flung himself down at her side and asked her which voyage she was reading.

"Captain Barlowe's first coming to Virginia."

"Give me the book," he said, reaching across for it. "I'll show you an even better bit."

But she saw his hands in time.

"Look at your hands!" she exclaimed, snatching the precious volume away. "Whatever is it?"

They were covered with a bright red dust.

"Nothing," he said sheepishly. "Just something I found at the back of the barn."

He wiped the stuff off on the grass. But he did not ask for the *Voyages* again. He sat beside her without speaking, gazing down upon the farmhouse and the river beyond. Both their thoughts were back with their father, ill unto death in an Oxfordshire farm, and with their mother journeying alone across England to help save his life.

At length Ralph told her about his leaving them in the morning.

"Uncle Ben wants to make the most of the ebb tide. The hoy'll be off our jetty at half-past three."

"Wake me up," she said. "I'll walk down with you."

It was a cobweb morning. Long scarves of mist lay over the river. There was not a breath of wind.

"Abe'll bring her in, very like," Ralph said, as they stood on the jetty.

Kate shivered. It was eerie in the deep silence before dawn, standing there far out above the water. Then, from the far side of the mist, she heard a faint plop in the river and a faint sigh of something moving down on the tide . . . then another plop.

"That's her," said Ralph softly.

And out of the haze loomed the *Essex Maid*.

He grasped Kate's hand. He would come back to her when he could, he said. He would try to come back for the harvest. Then, as the hoy glided past the end of the jetty, he leaped on board, turned for a second and waved, and then disappeared.

He was glad to be gone, she thought sadly, as she watched the stern of her uncle's ship fading away downstream, scarved in the mist. And no wonder. It would be easier for him pulling at ropes all day and unloading cheeses than staying here at High Ashfield.

She walked slowly back up to the farm, knowing that she was returning to an elder brother and sister whom she did not understand, to a season of grinding work, and to the long drawn-out waiting for news from their mother.

She was returning, too—though she did not know it—to Ralph's last fling at Mr. Pratt.

"Someone's painted the dragon's tongue scarlet!" Adam burst in upon them at breakfast.

She and Priscilla jumped up and ran out to look at it. There it was, a great scarlet lick, coming around the corner of the house and pointing at the beehive.

"Which of you did it?" demanded Priscilla angrily, turning on Kate.

But Adam—to her great surprise—suddenly burst out laughing. He must have guessed how it had been with Ralph.

"Perhaps it's one of Mr. Pratt's acts of God," he said.

Kate had been quite right about the season of grinding work. It was the very worst time in the year for them to have been left without their mother's help. There was the hay to rake and stack and cart away to the new-thatched hovels and preparations to be made for the harvest: grist to get ground at the miller's, the wagon to be overhauled, reaping hooks to be honed, pies baked— everything to be got ready against the long days that all three of them would have to spend in the harvest field. And all this was on top of their usual tasks. Adam and Smy had to sow the winter wheat, Priscilla to attend to the dairy work, and Kate, to the poultry and to the cutting of the flax.

Fifteen days later came their mother's first letter to Adam.

"Dear Son,
   The Lord be praised! Your father's fever is still strong upon—but he lives. May God preserve him. My blessing to you all.
                         Your mother.

Have it in mind that you should thatch the pigsty. Tell Priscilla to send the yarn to Mr. Hopkin. And keep Kate at her tasks. Pray for us."

"Well, we must pray—and work," said Adam grimly, putting down the letter. "That's all we *can* do."
   And pray and work they did.
   In the daze of her anxiety, Kate got the two confused in her mind.
   "If I finish the row of flax before noon," she told herself, "Father will live. If I finish the whole lot before dusk, then the fever will begin to leave him."

For a whole week, all three of them worked with a devotion that they never attained again.

The next news came up from the river and was brought by Ralph.

He came running up from the jetty and up through Wash Meadow with the letter open in his hand.

"Father's better! Father's better!" he shouted, as he ran into the farmyard.

They all came running toward him—Bet and old Smy as well.

"Uncle Ben opened it," he panted as he handed it to Adam.

The letter had been directed to Smart's Quay and told Adam that their father was indeed over the worst of his illness. The fever was slowly leaving him and his mind was clear. Their mother read to him from the Holy Book, she wrote. But his body was still weak. It might be a month until it was safe to have him carried into Essex.

"Thank God," said Adam simply.

And the old couple in their midst, forgetting the coming of the Puritans—who forbade such practices— crossed themselves in their thankfulness.

The hoy was waiting for Ralph off the jetty; so Kate ran down with him to see him off.

"Only another month, Kate," he grinned as she hugged him good-bye. "And we'll have him home. Home for always!"

But what a month!

If *only* their father had come home to them straightaway. If only he had!

Bartholomew's Eve

4

Yet, at the time, it was a lovely month. The danger was past. The sun shone. The wheat turned to gold. And for Kate that first morning, as she ran up to Langby to tell Tamsin their news, the whole world seemed newborn. A great burden had rolled off her back. She was filled with joy.

"I'm so glad for you," cried Tamsin, with the tears rolling down her face. "It's so terrible losing a father . . ."

And then she laughed and clasped Kate again.

"And now he's coming back to you . . . and . . . and I'll meet him at last"—which was loving of Tamsin, seeing that her own father had been killed fighting for the King.

"And Uncle Cooper will be back too, before very long," she went on. "Aunt says that now that Oxford has fallen and the fighting is finished, the Essex troopers are bound to be disbanded. Parliament knows how badly they are needed on the farms."

Poor Tamsin! And even poor futile, conceited

Simon! It would go hard with them both when Mr. Cooper returned.

Orphaned of both their parents in the first year of the war, they had been sent right across country from Cornwall to Essex to be brought up by their mother's sister and her husband at Langby. Mrs. Cooper had Tamsin's warm Cornish heart. But Mr. Cooper was a close man—so their mother said.

"Did Adam tell you what he and Simon have arranged about the harvest?" Tamsin asked.

"No."

"If the weather holds, we're all to start up here early next week. When we've finished, we'll come down to you."

The arrangements were much as they had been in other years, save that their mother and Mrs. Cooper had, in the past, made the decisions. But now that Adam and Simon were seasoned farmers of seventeen, they were clearly fit to arrange things themselves. The wheat that was ripest had to be harvested first. The Langby field was higher and sunnier than theirs down at High Ashfield.

Why then was that harvest tide so different?

Was it something new in Adam? In Simon? In Priscilla? In Tamsin? Or was it just the old people's chatter about the harvests of their youth? Or was it—as Kate came to think afterward—that all five of them, Adam, Simon, Priscilla, Tamsin, and herself, had just walked out of the valley of the shadow of their father's illness into the blazing sun?

The foreignness of Tamsin's beauty in that harvest field struck her all over again. Tamsin did not belong to Essex. She was far too vital and full of joy. Her black hair and the bright glow in her cheeks made the rest of them look quite pale. And, as though she were somehow enjoying her strangeness, she sang them one Cornish song after another as she bound the sheaves.

"They're lovely, Tamsin," Kate said. "But I wish I knew what they meant."

Tamsin looked across to her and her whole face suddenly shone with fun.

> "Yeghes da dhe'n Myghtern!
> Dew re-ngwyth-o gag col!" *

she sang triumphantly.

The words rang out across the flat Essex countryside.

"Oh, no, Tamsin! Not that one," shouted her brother, and then suddenly burst out laughing.

"Why, what does it mean?" Kate asked.

"I'll sing you another—a song in English," Tamsin replied quickly. "Then, when you've learned it, you can all join in."

And she sang them "John Dory."

> "As it fell on a holiday
> And upon a holy tide . . ."

By lunch time, Adam and Priscilla and Kate had mastered both words and part song and they sang out lustily, for Kate all sorrow gone, till she glanced across at her brother.

Is he *really* happy? flashed through her mind. Or is he just grabbing at this harvest joy?

After they had eaten, the five of them sat in the shadow of the hedge with the empty cider flagon and the broken meats lying on the grass beside them and sang again the brave ventures of Sir John Nichol and his Fowey gallants.

"Sam, bor," said Smy, when the last glorious chords had floated away between the corn shocks. "Don't it hev you in mind o' the ole days?"

---

* "Here's good Health to the King
May his foes from him fly!"

Mr. Dyer, the Coopers' hired man, smiled an ancient smile.

"Time ole Tom Ryder were cap'n o' the *Hawkey*?" he said, his eyes looking far away back into the past.

"Our grandfather?" asked Kate, pricking up her ears.

"Thet's hin, mawther."

"Tell us about him," she said impetuously. "Tell us everything you can."

Smy rubbed his hand through his hair in a puzzled way.

"En' much to tell, save he were a good, merry master."

"He liked his ale, ole Tom Ryder did," added Mr. Dyer.

"But he weren't never drunk, Sam," put in Bet sharply. "He were a good Christian soul . . ."

"Aye, an' he liked the ole country ways."

"Did he carry home the last wagonload of wheat with the flags and garlands as they used to do in Cornwall?" asked Tamsin.

"Thet we did," replied Mr. Dyer, warming to the happiness of times past. "An' blowin' on our pipes . . . an' singin' . . . an' all."

And slowly, in cracked voices and out of the sunlit memories of the old, the world of Merry England was born again.

"You danced around the maypole . . . and Grandfather, too?" asked Priscilla in shocked tones.

"We were young, then," put in old Bet, by way of excuse. "We were all of us young."

"And the maids really went a-wassailing at Christmas?" asked Adam in amusement.

"Thet you did, Bet," said Smy, digging his wife in the ribs. "And we lads fell to cudgelin' an' bobbin' for them hot apples . . ."

"Cudgeling? Not Sam, here!" jeered Simon, turning

to the bent old man and laughing unkindly. "Surely, Sam, you weren't ever much hand with a cudgel?"

"My Sam, he were a right stout fellow when he were a lad," rapped out Mrs. Dyer in angry defense.

"But the best time . . . the best time at High Ashfield," said Bet, carrying on the tale of times past. "It were at Saint Bartholomy's Wake."

"In them heathen times," Smy apologized for his wife, "our Bartholomy . . . he were called a saint."

On Saint Bartholomew's Eve, the old laborer said, the young people of the parish—the lasses and lads— used to watch all night in the Parish Church.

"Fine goings-on there were an' all," rumbled Mr. Dyer in ancient glee.

"Parson put an end on't even in our day," added Smy ruefully. "But he couldn't stop the feastin' on the feast day. Thet went on till . . . till the preachers showed us the sinfulness of our ways."

"And we all grew glum," Kate heard Adam mutter to himself.

Yet not one of them was glum that first day up at Langby. She, for herself, could scarcely remember a happier few hours. Had Ralph only been allowed to come to them, her joy would have spilled over. They sang in the field and they sang again as they walked back to the farmstead—Adam and Priscilla and Kate knowing that Mrs. Cooper had a better supper awaiting them than they had eaten since their mother had gone to their father. It was always thus at Langby. Tamsin's aunt knew how to feed her flock.

And then the two of them spoiled it all.

"Time you were off, Kate," Adam announced as soon as the table was cleared.

"Off?"

"You've got the poultry to feed," said Priscilla. "And there's the eggs to collect from along the hedge."

"Aren't . . . aren't you coming back, too?" she asked, hurt to the quick.

They were sending her away. They were shutting her out.

"We'll come later," said Adam. "Off you go—and hurry. It'll be dark in another half hour."

She stood up in the Langby kitchen, hot-faced and rebellious.

"Why couldn't you have got Bet to do the poultry when she did the milking?"

"Because the hens are your job," Priscilla smacked back.

"And the milking's yours."

"Hurry, Kate," said Adam. "You know how you hate the dark."

She flushed even deeper. Her shame was out. She was afraid of going home by herself.

"Yes, Kate's afraid of the dark," mocked Priscilla.

Humiliated in front of them all, she fled, choking with angry tears.

"Wait for me, Kate," Tamsin shouted after her. "I'll go with you past the great stone."

She heard them all shouting for Tamsin not to leave them . . . and then her friend's footsteps close behind.

"I . . . I was afraid of the dark, too, when I was young," Tamsin panted as she caught up.

When they were close to the farm, she added gently, "It's just the same world, Kate, as it is by day. The trees are the same and the hedges and puddles. The only thing that's different is that the sun's gone."

Kate shivered and said nothing. She knew that the world was not at all the same. With the going of the sun, it was filled with evil. The trees stood and leered and bent down their twigs to catch in one's hair. Bats flitted over one's head; at least, she always hoped they were bats—but she feared that they were the spells of the

43

witches winging their way to do harm. Even the earth itself was different, for certain fields spawned wickedness, just as others, more innocently, sprouted white mushrooms.

Still, it was kind of Tamsin to understand. She reached out and took her hand to tell her so. It was kinder still of her to walk with her past the great boulder at the top of the lane. She had not realized up to now that Tamsin had guessed with what terror she herself had endowed the famous Langby stone.

Two winters ago they had talked about old superstitions as they sat roasting apples in the hot ashes of Mrs. Cooper's hearth.

"In the West Country," Tamsin had said, laughing, "the old people used to fear a certain hobgoblin who looked just like a rock covered with hair. He would wait for his victims silently, nothing moving—not even his eyes."

"A rock covered with hair!" Kate had gulped in horror, suddenly seeing the hobgoblin quite clearly pretending to be the Langby stone.

In the dusk of that harvest night, they skirted around the dreadful stone and came out onto the village green.

"Look," said Tamsin. "There's still a faint light in the west. You'll get those hens fed and shut up before it's completely dark. And once inside one's own house, it's always quite safe."

They bid each other good-bye.

Sick of heart and ashamed for her cowardice, Kate ran down the familiar lane.

"Quite safe?" she muttered. "Dear Lord, I hope it is. I hope it is!"

She had never before returned alone to an empty home. She had always been with Ralph or Priscilla or Adam; and their mother had been waiting there to welcome them out of the dark with a taper or a glowing fire. Tonight there would be no one. No light. No sound. In her panic haste to get back to High Ashfield and to face what had to be faced, she ran up on the hedge bank to cut off a corner.

And then it happened.

An unseen hand from under the earth grasped her harshly by the right ankle—and suddenly the brambles and bracken and dew-soaked grass were hurled up into her face. She was down on the hard ground, gasping, sobbing, the handclasp around her leg tightening into a stabbing pain.

"Dear Lord protect me!" she wept into the wet grass.

Old Raw-Head and Bloody-Bones must have stalked underground right into the heart of Essex to drag her down into his lair.

And then, with her face still buried in the undergrowth, she heard her mother's voice as crisply as though she were standing over her there in the Ashfield lane.

"Don't be a fool, Kate," it said. "You've put your foot down a rabbit hole and you've twisted your ankle. Lift it out gently, roll over onto your back, and try to make yourself comfortable."

She did as she was told. The ankle hurt so much when she moved it that she wanted to cry out with the pain. But, instead, she stuffed the side of her hand into her mouth and bit hard. It was better to make no noise. Safer. The evil presences in the night might pass her by unnoticed if she made no sound. They might think she was just a shadow or the fallen branch of a tree, lying there silently on the hedge bank. She lay a long time with her hand in her mouth, staring up at the darkening sky and praying that Adam and Priscilla would come to her soon, while all the time her leg throbbed and burned as though someone had tied it too tight with a rope. Slowly, the thousand small noises of the country night stole back into the quietness. The wind creaked gently in the brambles. Two fields off—in the High Meadow—a sheep coughed. Close at hand, a late rabbit hopped over the cart rut in the lane and grazed anxiously on the raised mound of the wheel spur. She watched its white scut with affection. The creature looked so innocent, snatching its last nibble before the dark.

Tired out by the pain and the long day in the harvest field, she lay and watched the rabbit, the weight of her own cowardice heavy upon her. Where now was Sir Francis Drake's intrepid companion? What would Job Hortop and Captain Barlowe—and her own father —think of her now?

In her misery, she must have dropped off to sleep.

When next she looked up at the sky, it was quite dark. Overhead there was neither moon nor stars, only a slowly moving mantle of clouds. She shivered. With so much cloud about it might mizzle before dawn.

And then, at the thought of the dawn, she was in a panic again. Adam and Priscilla might have come down from Langby while she slept and not noticed her lying on the bank. She might have to lie out in the open here all night, a helpless prey to the Devil's Dandy dogs, breathing fire, or to Tatterfoal, the goblin horse, or to Galley-Beggar, the headless ghost. By daylight she knew that these were fireside tales, told by Tamsin and Bet to make one shiver and then laugh; but at night, alone in the lane . . . without a moon . . .

And then something soft bumbled into her face, and she gasped.

"Don't be a baby, Kate," said her mother sternly. "It's not a ghost, it's a moth . . ."

Her mother's voice went on and on, sharp and clear as it always did, ". . . and if you really think the others have passed you by, then be sensible and slither down the bank and lie in the middle of the lane. You'll be easier to find when they come back looking for you . . ."

Kate did what she said, thinking gratefully, through

the stabbing pain in her ankle as she slid down the bank, how clever it was of her mother to be reading the Holy Book to her father in an Oxfordshire farm and yet at the same time to be here in the Ashfield lane, chiding her to use her wits.

"And now that you're lying comfortably in the middle of the path, do—for the Lord's sake—put your mind to rights. No more of your childishness. Begin reciting the Twenty-third Psalm."

And this she did.

The words were a great comfort to her because they made her smile.

Well, she thought without irreverence, the Lord really has made me "to lie down in green pastures."

And then, as she went on through the psalm, she saw the force of her mother's wisdom.

" 'Yea, though I walk through the valley of the shadow of death,' " she murmured, " 'I will fear no evil, for Thou art with me . . .' "

And then—almost immediately—it was not only the Almighty who was with her but also Adam and Priscilla.

With a stab of anger, she listened to them singing the chorus of "John Dory" as they came down from Langby through the darkness.

In the cold glimmer of dawn it was clear to all three of them that she had sprained her ankle badly.

"I'd have thought you might've been trusted not to blunder about in the dark like that," Adam sighed wearily as he surveyed her blue-and-purple foot. "It looks as though it'll take weeks to heal."

"I'm sorry, Adam," she said, understanding his vexation. "I really am . . ."

"I expect you are," he replied with a wry smile. "It looks as though it hurts."

"You've made yourself useless," snapped Priscilla. "Just when you might've been some help."

Kate bit her lip. She hated her sister.

Adam had carried her in from the lane last night and laid her down on a sheepskin on the floor of the house-room.

"Goodness knows what you're going to do all day," Priscilla went on, running in with her breakfast. "Card some wool, I suppose. I'll set it by you before we go."

"I'll get Mrs. Cooper to come to you, Kate," said Adam, frowning again at the discolored sprain. "She'll know what's best to be done for that swelling."

When they had gone, she lay listening to the hens clucking in the farmyard outside and ached with hurt pride. Last night up at Langby they had sent her off cruelly, longing to be rid of her. She was too young—for anybody except Ralph ever to want. And now, this morning, she was imprisoned here by her foot. She gazed at her mother's painted cloth of Naomi and Ruth becoming every minute more detailed and distinct in the growing light and felt the bitterness of her exclusion. They were all at the harvest—at the most joyful labor of the year: Tamsin, Simon, Priscilla, Adam—and even Naomi and Ruth and Boaz over there on the wall. She alone was shut out.

A fear shot up into the open that morning as frightening as the goblin's hand that had plucked her down the rabbit hole last night. Was she—Kate—always to be shut out? Was she destined to live her life alone—and without reward? Unlike Adam, she could not inherit the fields in which they all worked so hard. Unlike Ralph, she could not sail away and join the great explorers. Unlike Priscilla and Tamsin, she might not marry. She was not pretty. Was hoeing peas and carding wool here at High Ashfield all that life held for a girl like herself?

Then she thought of her parents. Would her mother's coming home make things better? She loved her mother. But she thought not. And her father? He was a shining knight, a hero. But he was a stranger. It came to her in a panic that the stranger might not like his youngest child whom he found waiting for him at home. He had loved her once. But she had changed in four years. She knew that she had changed.

Waiting, worn out and miserable, for Mrs. Cooper to come, she saw no comfort anywhere in the world.

But she had reckoned without Tamsin.

Two hours later Tamsin's aunt called Kate's name as she walked through the farmyard.

"I'm here in the house-room, Mrs. Cooper," she called back.

She sat up listlessly, waiting for their kind neighbor to let herself in through the kitchen and appear in the doorway. Instead, came a smothered laugh and a scuffle of sharp feet; and—to her astonishment—in bounded one of Tamsin's bitch puppies.

"It's Molly!" she exclaimed, beginning to smile. "Or is it Polly?"

"It's Polly," replied Mrs. Cooper, following behind. "And, if you'd like her, she's come to stay."

"To *stay?*"

"Our Tamsin's that sorry for what's happened, Kate; she thought you'd like to have the little thing."

"For *always?*" she asked thickly.

Mrs. Cooper nodded and then settled herself down on a stool at her side to look at her ankle.

A great love for Tamsin swept up from Kate's heart—and a great love for this warm, wriggling piece of life now sitting on her chest. The love was so overwhelming that the tears started up in her eyes. One rolled down her cheek. The puppy poked forward and licked it away.

Mrs. Cooper grasped her swollen ankle with cool hands and felt about along the bones.

"The Lord be praised!" she said, at last. "Nothing's broken. But it's a cruel wrench. No wonder you're crying."

Kate smiled through the tears and kept her secret. The puppy had now bumped against her nose and fallen off sideways onto the floor.

"I don't know what your mother will say," Mrs. Cooper went on, as she began binding the ankle up tightly in strips of clean cloth. "The little thing's not properly clean yet in the house . . ."

Kate knew this already. A warm trickle was running down her ribs.

". . . So you'll have to be quick about the training before your parents come home."

Kate nodded, scarcely listening, for her whole being was reaching out and growing gentle with love for the puppy. Polly was to be her own. Not her mother's, not Adam's, not Priscilla's—but *hers*, Kate's.

"And now we must get you a pair of crutches," said Tamsin's aunt, as she finished the bandaging. "You've got to walk about and use that foot just as much as you can bear it."

"Walk?" she exclaimed in alarm.

"That's it, Kate," Mrs. Cooper said firmly. "It's best for the ankle—and it's best for you."

She could not stay here lying on the house-room floor all day right through the harvest, she went on sternly. It was not healthy or right. Adam must make her some crutches, and he and Priscilla must put her into the cart tomorrow morning and bring her up to Langby. She could lie by the hedge and watch them cut the wheat.

Mrs. Cooper stooped down and drew a wedge of pie out of her basket. Then, turning back to her patient, she paused, peering down at her anxiously.

"You look whittery, Kate. Shall I take that puppy away with me—just for the day—so you can get some

sleep? Tamsin's coming tonight with your supper. She could bring her back."

"No," she cried, reaching out for Polly in a panic.

Mrs. Cooper smiled.

"Well, I expect the two of you'll do each other good duddled up together. But eat your lunch before I go. Quick now, while I fetch you both some milk."

And so it was that Kate became a looker-on at the harvest.

She lay on the hedge bank in the first days, lost in her joy of the puppy now tumbling about in the long grass at her side, now dashing out incautiously into the sharp stubble, and now returning for comfort and laying

51

her muzzle in her lap. A whole new world of tenderness had been suddenly revealed to her. She felt gentler, calmer, more at peace with her lot. She heard the bees buzzing about her in the summer flowers and the voices of the reapers calling to one another deep in the wheatfield and was content to be just Kate: Kate alone with her Polly.

Every now and again, Tamsin gave over binding Simon's sheaves and sat beside her, companionable and loving, talking to them both.

It was enough.

Then, as her ankle grew stronger, she slowly came back to the problems of High Ashfield.

Gazing at her brother one day, she caught him, unawares, pausing for a moment from his reaping, with the same tortured look in his bearing that she had seen from afar on the day of the clipping.

His trouble had not gone away. He might sing Tamsin's songs with them all. He might laugh at their jokes. He and Priscilla might spend every evening up at Langby and return home roistering, long after dark. But he was still unhappy. He was still torn by some unknown grief.

Then, one day, she saw in a flash how it *really* was.

They had finished cutting and shocking the wheat up at Langby and had been working for the past two days in their own field at High Ashfield; and since they were working on Ryder land, Adam was now captain of the harvest. As captain, he allowed himself a pause every ten minutes or so to look about him to see how the work was going forward.

From her hedge bank, Kate gazed drowsily at her brother during one of these pauses—and suddenly shot wide awake.

He was not unhappy, not drawn away into his own thoughts. He was standing, looking across the top of the

waving wheat at Tamsin, his whole being absorbed in his
gaze. What she saw in his face turned her quiet world
upside down. He was smoldering, glowing—about to
burst into flame—with love. Adam! Tamsin! She was
filled with astonished dismay. Then she looked across at
her friend. Tamsin was stooping, her face turned away
from Adam, binding her brother's sheaf and at the same
time telling Simon a story that was making him
laugh.

Then she glanced back at her brother. There was no
mistaking the deep passion in his gaze.

Dear heavens! she thought aghast. Ralph was quite
wrong. It's not Tamsin who's looking for a husband. It's
Adam . . . who's found his bride!

All day she kept her discovery to herself, hidden away. But that night, alone in the house, she took it out and looked at it again—and felt an even greater dismay. Tamsin was fifteen. Only fifteen. She was a Royalist. Without parents. Without a penny in the world. She was the last girl in Essex whom her parents would accept as Adam's bride.

"Poor little Tamsin," her mother had once said. "I don't know who the Coopers can get to marry her, seeing that she has no portion to bring to her husband."

Poor Tamsin. Poor Adam.

She longed for her parents to come home quickly and put an end to Adam's breaking heart.

That Sunday Kate left a bewildered Polly chained up in Trash's old kennel and limped to church between her brother and sister, glad to be walking again even in this miserable fashion and relieved that they were returning at least to the outward pattern of their old ways. There would be no gadding over to Langby tonight. Surely not. The three of them would sit in the house-room—as on other Sabbaths—and Adam would read to them from the Holy Book. He had a fine voice and he chose passages that she loved: Noah's flood, David killing Goliath, Elijah being fed by the ravens. It would be a happy evening, sitting on the floor, fondling Polly, and listening to such tales.

But it was not to be.

"Come along, Priscilla," Adam shouted up to her as dusk was falling. "Surely you've done decking yourself in ribbons."

"You're not going out?" Kate asked in astonishment. "It's . . . it's the Sabbath. . . ."

"It's something else besides the Sabbath," Priscilla threw at her with a laugh as she arrived at the bottom of the stairs.

"Come along," said Adam impatiently, pushing her

54

out through the kitchen. "And you go to bed early, Kate. I'll expect a little work out of you tomorrow in the harvest field."

Something else?

She sat on in the shadows, remembering sullenly what that "something" was. It was August 23—Bartholomew's Eve. Mr. Pratt had made a passing allusion to the apostle after whom the church had been named. Bartholomew had been faithful unto death, he had told them, and unto death should they too be faithful, should the Lord send them that test.

And all that old Bartholomew means to Adam and Priscilla and Simon and Tamsin, she thought spitefully, is to go larking about in his church all night.

Then she reproved herself for envy. If only Ralph had been here, he and she and Polly would have gone up to the church, too. She was sure they would.

She awoke hours later from a deep sleep to someone knocking loudly on the front door. Polly was growling bravely under the coverlid.

"Master Ryder . . . Master Adam Ryder," shouted a boy's voice.

Kate ran to her mother's bedroom window with the puppy barking and tumbling over her feet.

"What is it?" she called down when she had opened the casement.

"Is this Goodman Ryder's farm . . . Goodman John Ryder's?"

"Yes."

"There's a message from 'en for his son . . . his son Adam."

"Yes. Yes. What is it?"

"The master o' the *Essex Maid*—we hailed 'en in the dark off Osyth Point . . . waitin' for the tide. He's a-bringin' Goodman Ryder an' his wife upriver . . . just as soon as ever there's enough water. He says hev the horse waitin' at the jetty . . . and . . . and put the best linen on the parlor bed . . ."

"Goodness!" shouted Kate in delight. "They'll be here in a few hours."

"Give 'en three," said the boy. "The tide . . . she's swellin' fast."

"I'll come down and let you in," she said.

But no. He had to be off, back to the river, he replied. His master was waiting for him in the smack off the jetty. They had to be up to Colchester with their catch before dawn.

"What's the time now?"

"Past two o'clock."

Past two o'clock, she thought astonished, as she dragged on her clothes in the darkness. And where were Adam and Priscilla? Not still at Bartholomew's Church? She ran down into the kitchen with the puppy flattening herself on the floor and then jumping up against her bare legs, barking in a fever of excitement.

"Thank goodness for you, Polly," she said aloud, as she let them both out into the darkness of the farmyard. "You'll frighten the wits out of the night things."

Just past the gate into the High Meadow, she saw a figure coming toward her, a girl, her dress palely white in the darkness. She had ribbons in her hair. It was Priscilla.

"Priscilla," she shouted to the figure ahead. "Mother and Father . . . they'll be home in three hours. Uncle Ben's got them aboard the *Essex Maid*."

Priscilla, who was level with her now, gave a sort of gulp.

"What's happened?" Kate asked in amazement. "Why are you crying?"

Priscilla's shoulders shook with her weeping.

"It was just a stupid game," she burst out in angry tears. "A hateful, wicked game."

Kate stared at her sister, uncomprehending. What

was stupid? What was wicked? Why was she not joyful and excited that their parents were coming home?

"Where's Adam?" she asked.

"In the churchyard . . . with Tamsin."

"Please run back and tell him about Mother and Father . . ."

"No," howled Priscilla.

"But you can get up to the churchyard quicker than I can."

"No. No. I won't."

And her sister fled past her down the lane toward the house, crying aloud as she went.

Kate stared after her, nonplussed.

When she had limped painfully through the village and come to the churchyard wall, she saw Adam and Tamsin sitting on Sir Matthew Paycocke's tomb.

They were a single, dark shadow, unmoving, unseeing—as heedless as a gravestone. Awed by their silence, Kate limped up the churchyard path and came up quite close. Adam had his arm around Tamsin's waist. Tamsin's head was resting against his sleeve. Their stillness was uncanny. It was as though they had been bewitched and turned to stone.

She took a step nearer, and Polly—sensing her former young mistress—struggled in her arms, jumped to the ground, and ran with little soft barks of joy to Tamsin's feet.

Tamsin stirred gently, with her head still resting where it was. She stirred as one stirs in a dream.

"Polly," she murmured, smiling. "And Kate."

Adam looked at them both as though he, too, had traveled from far away.

"Adam," Kate burst out. "Father and Mother are coming home. They'll be down at the jetty in less than three hours. Uncle Ben's bringing them."

Her brother frowned a little in perplexity, as though he could not quite grasp what she was saying.

"Your father and mother, Adam," Tamsin said dreamily, still smiling. "They're coming home."

Then he woke up—and was almost himself again.

"Take your puppy, Kate," he said quietly, as they both stood up, "and start walking home. I'll be with you in a minute."

Kate looked back on them from the churchyard wall. Adam was kissing Tamsin full on the lips—not hungrily or wantonly as she had seen couples kiss at the Colchester fair—but soberly and reverently, as though he were putting his seal to a bond.

"Take Kate up on your shoulders," Tamsin called after him as he strode away. "She's tired with that ankle. She's as light as a sparrow."

The Return

5

A cold dawn heralded their parents' homecoming. A squall was blowing up the valley from the sea. The light when it came, low in the east, peered a greenish-yellow through bars of black cloud. It was not the bright dawn that it should have been, Kate thought as she hugged Polly close to her under her cloak. The whole firmament should have been flying banners to welcome their father. The sky and the river should have been scarlet with light. Instead, the water slapped sullenly under the jetty, greenish-yellow and pitted with rain. Behind them, his beloved High Ashfield, his fields and barns and the farmstead itself, was hidden in shadow and dripping with water.

"We ought to have lit a bonfire," she burst out. "A huge bonfire in the middle of the High Meadow."

Adam nodded absently, still half lost in his dream.

"It would have gone out in this rain," shivered Priscilla drearily, pulling her hood closer down over her hair.

Kate glanced at her sister's pinched, unhappy face

59

and at her brother's drawn one and turned from them in
anger. She could not bear it that they were less excited
than herself. She could not understand their lack of joy.
After four long years, they were all to have a father
again—their own father, a hero, a good man! Today, a
whole new era was beginning in their lives.

"There she is," said Adam quietly.

"Where? Where?" she burst out, spinning around.

"You can see her pennon and the tip of her sail . . .
there . . . look just to the left of the old mill."

As so often in that flat valley, the ship looked as
though it were sailing toward them over dry land.

"She's on the port tack," he said. "When she enters
our reach, she'll have the wind straight behind her."

The squall blew off a little, and a weak ray of
sunshine filtered across the *Essex* waste just as the hoy
entered Wash Meadow reach.

That's braver. That's braver, she thought, her heart
thumping with excitement as the *Essex Maid* bore down
toward them, her red sail stretched out almost the width
of the river, and the reeds on the far bank billowing in
her heavy wake. That's how a hero should come home.

She could see Ralph standing up in the prow. He
waved at her. She waved back. She scanned the ship, but
there was no sign of their mother or father. They must be
below in the cabin—out of the rain. The hoy was coming
up at a spanking pace.

Ralph put his hands to his mouth, cupping them,
and shouted, "Adam, we're sailing up beyond you . . .
and then turning back into the wind. Stand ready to
catch a rope."

Adam nodded.

The *Essex Maid* swept past them. And in the second
of her passing, Kate caught a glimpse of a gaunt,
white-haired man dressed in a torn leather buff coat,
standing beside her mother in the cabin door. For an
amazed moment, she could not think who it could be.

Then the hoy turned in a tremendous churning of water and loud flapping of empty sail. Abe, the older apprentice, had the quant pole out and began edging the hoy against wind and tide toward the end of the jetty.

It was not at all as she had thought it would be.

Childishly, she had expected her hero to ride back into their lives with the same fine flourish with which he had ridden out of them. She had not remembered his going. She had not remembered him as a plain, everyday man, as her mother's husband, as Adam and Priscilla and Ralph's father—as well as her own. She was in no way prepared for the moving ordinariness of what took place on the jetty.

Uncle Ben and Ralph helped the white-haired man over the gunwale of the *Essex Maid*, and he walked over to the three of them kneeling there on the planking, awaiting his blessing.

"Adam," he said hoarsely, laying a hand on his head. "My thanks and my blessing. May God reward you for being so good a son."

As Adam rose and stammered out his greeting, Kate saw that he was taller than their father and broader and much stronger.

Priscilla had thrown back her hood. Her hair glimmered palely gold in the early light.

"And Priscilla . . . ," he said. "God bless you."

He raised her up and kissed her tenderly on the forehead and then stood scanning her face with an amused kind of wonder.

"Why, I left my daughter a child . . . and see, now . . . why, she is a maid well-nigh ripe for a husband."

Kate heard her sister give another of her gulps.

"You're looking right green-sickly, child," said their mother sharply. "What ails you? And you, too, Adam? You both look as though you had not been to bed for weeks . . ."

Their father had moved on and had come now to

herself. She could feel the light touch of his hand on her hair.

"And this must be my little scholar," he said, laughing gently.

And the stranger who was no stranger raised her up and kissed her and then stood back, taking in slowly what kind of being it was he had in his youngest child.

"Well, Kate," he said, smiling, "I'll have to learn about you all over again."

"And I, you," she blurted out.

Then she went scarlet with grief. He would think she was mocking his white hair and his poor shrunken body; he would guess that she could scarcely remember him at all.

But instead of being angry, he startled her with a round, happy laugh.

"What . . . and a puppy, too?"

She glanced down quickly. Polly had escaped from her cloak. She was standing at her father's feet, looking up as though she, too, ought to have his blessing.

"Good Lord, Kate!" burst out Ralph. "That's one of Tamsin's little bitches, isn't it?"

"Polly's mine, now," she threw back straight at Ralph—but aiming her defiance at her mother.

They helped their father up onto old Steadfast. And then Uncle Ben, catching Ralph by the ear, bid them all good-bye.

"I'll send this urchin back to you tonight, John, when we've unloaded her cargo," he said. "But I'll want him down here on the river by Tuesday's ebb tide."

In the last flurry of the storm, the old cavalry horse ambled up the lane bearing his master slowly home, while the four of them plodded on through the dying squall at their father's side, dripping with rain. Everything was dripping: the elm trees overhead, the bracken fronds at their feet, the brambles, the bars of the gates into the meadows.

"Put your cloak about your face, John," said their
mother in her sharp, urgent way. And then, turning to
Priscilla: "The bed's aired as I sent word?"

Kate glanced at her father and saw that he was not
doing what he was told. Instead, he had turned his head
seaward and was taking great breathfuls of damp air into
his lungs.

"It smells good, Margaret," he said by way of
excuse. "It smells good to be home."

Kate's heart gave a lurch. This stranger who was no
stranger knew the joys of High Ashfield quite as well she
did; he loved the scorched tang of summer rain on the
dry earth and the sweet freshness blowing off wet bracken
fronds and bramble leaves. And, knowing this, her
childishness about her father suddenly fell away from

her, and she saw him for what he was: not a shining knight, not a hero of romance, but a tired-out Essex yeoman coming home to his own.

To his own? To Adam and Tamsin? To Priscilla? To herself?

She glanced at him again. He was looking eagerly first this way and then that at his sodden, familiar fields.

"It'll blow off before noon, Adam," he said cheerfully. "Never you fear."

"Dear Lord," she prayed silently, sensing all the trouble that lay ahead and crossing her fingers under Polly's warm belly. "I wish it would."

That dripping August morning, overjoyed at his coming home, her father dismounted painfully from old Steadfast in the farmyard and, despite their mother's anguished pleading, took Adam's arm and walked around his steading. He approved of the new thatch on the barn and walked into the barn to find Bet at the milking and stayed talking with her far longer than even Kate thought needful, asking her after Smy and their cottage and the health of their pig and for such small news of the village as Bet, of old, loved to tell, until their mother—exasperated beyond self-control—reminded him roundly that he was wet to the skin.

"You must bear with me, Margaret," he replied, smiling. "I have been waiting for this morning for four long years."

He said it firmly as though forbidding her to say more.

Then they trooped in a slow procession toward the pigsties where they found Smy carting away muck. And the greetings and the talk began again.

"Priscilla," their mother whipped out. "Go stoke up the kitchen fire, lay out that old shift of your father's . . . put fresh coals in the warming pan . . . put a skillet of milk to heat. For God's sake make the house *warm*."

Then the three who were left followed his limping

progress through the herb garden and along the flower plot to the front of the house, where he stopped for a moment by the dovecot, listening to the crooning welcome of the doves and gazing through the shifting veils of low cloud at his grazing sheep.

"You have done well," he murmured to Adam. "You have done well, my son, by our inheritance."

And then, coughing a little, he moved on toward the corner of the house.

Kate tugged gently at his arm.

"Look, Father," she said, pointing up to the carving of St. George. "You must see what Ralph has done to the dragon's tongue."

He laughed between sputters of coughing and asked why the boy had not finished his task.

"John," their mother broke in, beside herself with anxiety. "I fear for thee. I am afraid. Come in now, I beg you. Come into your home and take off your wet clothes."

Her fear was well-founded.

That same evening their father had a return of his fever. For a whole week he lay in the parlor bed, shivering and shaking under the linen sheet and the heaped-up blankets as though he were frozen to the bone, and then throwing off the coverings, declaring that he was burning hot and that his dear ones were killing him by their kindness.

Kate could read his danger in their mother's face and in the gentle way that she addressed them all, begging them for God's sake, and for the love they bore their father, to do this or that.

Slowly, slowly their father mended. His fever left him—and he slept.

Their mother became again their mother.

She left the invalid to sleep and busied herself in the

house. She looked about her in her dairy and her brewhouse, cast her eye along the dulled pewter cooking pots, and scowled in disgust at her kitchen floor, reading at a glance the weeks of misrule at High Ashfield while she had been away.

"Priscilla! Kate!" she rated them. "The house is a disgrace!"

Her anger scalded their pride. She had found rancid butter in the churn; the pewter was dirty and the pans unscoured . . . and one of them had burned a hole through her favorite skillet. What was she to do with such good-for-nothing daughters? Their father would be finding them suitors in a very few years. But how were they to cherish a husband—let alone win one—if they could do no better than this?

"And you, Priscilla, especially," their mother went on. "It is shameful! You are all of sixteen!"

Her sister railed bitterly against their mother in bed that night, saying that she was tired of moiling and toiling here at High Ashfield for someone so cross and ungrateful as their mother.

Worse was to come.

The next evening their mother discovered that she—Kate—had done no carding of wool.

"None at all, Kate?" she exclaimed, hardly believing her ears. "No carding of wool in eight whole weeks? But what did you do here in the evenings with that sprained ankle of yours?"

Kate looked down on the floor and let the question lose itself in the house-room shadows. She could not confess that Polly and her father's books had left her little time for carding wool, for her mother—in her anger— might well banish both from her life.

"And if Kate's carded no wool, Priscilla, it means you've been idle with your spinning. So what's happened to the yarn for Master Hopkin?"

Priscilla shrugged her shoulders.

"But I *told* you about it, child! I wrote to Adam, reminding you of the yarn. If you've sold no yarn, what are we to do for money to buy cloth for your father's coat?"

She was exasperated beyond measure.

"We sent some at first," Priscilla snapped. "Didn't we, Kate? And then came the harvest."

"The harvest! The harvest!" their mother retorted. She was always hearing about the harvest. But they had spun enough yarn at other harvest times, Priscilla and herself.

To Kate's consternation, Priscilla suddenly lost all self-control.

"We're *tired* of it, Mother," she shouted. "We're all tired of it. We've worked for you, spun for you, reaped for you, dug for you, plowed for you . . . ."

"For *me?*" exclaimed their mother in astonishment.

"For *you*. We've spent our whole lives breaking our backs on this hateful farm. It's too much. You . . . you take all."

"But we are a *family!*" protested their mother, too shocked to be angry. "Each works for the rest."

"It's not true, Mother. We children . . . we have to work for our parents. Look at Kate in her rags. Look at Adam . . . ."

"Dear Lord, make her stop," Kate prayed, scarlet with remorse, knowing that her sister was only blurting out aloud what she herself had so recently thought. "Please, please make her stop!"

But the Lord failed her.

"Look at Adam," Priscilla stormed on. "Do you think he's happy drudging away on his father's farm?"

"*Stop* it!" ordered their mother.

Into the silence that followed dropped the gentlest voice that a man can use.

"Priscilla, my child . . . ."

67

The three of them swung around in surprise. Kate had forgotten their father in bed in the parlor. He was standing now in the doorway—a strangely commanding figure in his night-shift.

"Priscilla, my dear, you are troubled in your mind. Come in quietly to me and tell me what it is."

But Priscilla shook her head wildly, put her hands to her face, and ran weeping up the stairs to their bedroom.

"I don't know what's happened to her while I've been away," her mother burst out. "She's always been fretful. But now she's downright . . ."

"She's growing up, my dear," answered her father with a sad humorous sigh. "They are all growing up."

Kate gathered Polly into her arms and held her tight for comfort, while her mother took her father back to bed.

"It's been a hard war for them, too," she heard her father say.

"It's been no such thing, John," she heard her mother reply tartly. "It's you that have had all the hurts . . . not they."

Kate knew vaguely that her mother was wrong. All four of them had received hurts from the hard work and the war. And that night as she lay in bed with her sister, she realized for the first time that Priscilla's hurt had perhaps been much greater than her own.

Her sister was still sobbing wretchedly when she came up to her. Her father, she wept, had spoken of finding her a husband in a few years. She prayed to God that he would find her one in a few months . . . in a few weeks. She could not endure their life here at High Ashfield.

"It's only because Mother's angry," Kate said, trying to console her.

"No, it's not. It's everyone."

"Not Adam . . . or Tamsin . . . or Simon," Kate protested, greatly bewildered. "You were all so happy at the harvest."

But Priscilla burst out weeping again with such bitterness that Kate was even more nonplussed.

And then she remembered her sister's tears in the lane—and a terrible fear for her shot in her mind.

"What happened in the church?" she blurted out. "Was it . . . was it that Simon . . . ?"

Priscilla buried her sobs in the pillow.

Kate looked at her—appalled by her fear.

"Priscilla," she whispered, dragging away the pillow. "You . . . you aren't going to have . . . have a baby?"

"A baby?" exclaimed her sister, so astonished that she sat bolt upright and stopped crying.

Then she blushed crimson.

"Of course not," she said angrily. "How could you think such a thing?"

It was Kate's turn to blush.

Then what had happened?

"Why are you so upset, then?" she asked, feeling childishly confused.

"Because he . . . he wanted . . . and I wanted . . ." stammered her sister, her lip trembling and a tear rolling down her cheek. ". . . And then . . . then I knew I . . . I didn't love him . . . didn't even *like* him."

Kate was swept with relief.

"He's no good," went on her sister. "He's got no money. No inheritance. Nothing. I . . . I don't think . . . he . . . he even cares for *me*."

Kate listened to the miserable little story, still sorely confused.

"He was so angry," said poor Priscilla, weeping

afresh. "So rough with me . . . when I pushed him away."

As he grew better, Kate spent more and more of her time in the parlor with her father. It seemed the most natural place for her to be.

"Kate, read to me," he requested, one evening when her work on the farm was done.

"From the Holy Book?" she replied, jumping up eagerly from carding her wool.

"No, child," he said, smiling at her in amusement. "Find one of the books that we used to read."

She went to the shelf and peered up at the few, precious books.

"Malory's *Morte d'Arthur*?" she suggested. "Ralph and I . . . we used to like his stories when we were young."

"No. Not old Malory. I'm weary of fighting, Kate. Weary of wars. Read me something about what men do when they're at peace."

"Foxe's *Book of Martyrs*?" she asked doubtfully.

"Dear God, child, are thumbscrews and the rack and the stake the instruments of peace?"

His anger was so sudden that it made her jump.

The next two books were books of sermons by Tobias Crisp and John Archer. If he did not want the Bible, he would not want them. And the next book after that was Thomas Tusser's *Five Hundred Points of Good Husbandry*. She passed this by, too. Her father might like it after his years of fighting, but she would not. Its tiresome, jingling rhymes were all about ordinary, dull farmwork. And she had had enough of that for one day.

"That only leaves Hakluyt's *Voyages*, Father. What about them?"

The tone of her voice must have given her away.

"They'll do," he said, smiling. "Since they're what you want yourself."

She picked Polly out of the carded wool, plumped
her—all flecked with white—on top of her father's bed,
and then sat down on the floor and reached hungrily for
the books.

"Where shall we go?" she asked, thumbing quickly
through the pages. "To Guinea with Sir John Hawkins?
Or . . . or to the Arctic with John Davis? Or . . . or
. . . what about around the world with Sir Francis
Drake?"

"You choose."

"Well, I like the Virginia bit about banging off the
harquebus and . . . the flock of cranes. But Ralph . . .
he likes things that happened to Miles Phillips in the
West Indies . . . and how he finally escaped from the
Spaniards' bloody hands."

"Goodness! Is *this* where you've both been all these
years?"

And then suddenly—because this mild stranger in
the bed was her father and because he did not mock her
or treat her as a child—out it all tumbled: the dream
that she had never told anyone in the world, not even
Ralph, the dream that she herself knew could never
really come true.

"Wouldn't it be wonderful, Father, if we could sail away in the *Essex Maid* and see all these places . . . really *see* the red cedars of Virginia and the goodly woods full of deer and conies and hares . . . and really *smell* the lovely smell that blows off the land . . ."

Her father did not laugh. For a brief moment he seemed caught up in the dream himself.

"Well, I suppose it's not impossible, Kate," he said thoughtfully. "After all, the Winthrops over in Suffolk did it fifteen years ago. But they went farther north."

"Oh! But I didn't mean as a family," she blurted out—and then blushed with distress, realizing what she had said.

"Just Ralph and yourself?" he asked gently.

She nodded.

"But Ralph's only a seaman apprentice. And the *Essex Maid* . . . well, she's only a little boat, Kate. She wouldn't get you far beyond Land's End."

It was said so understandingly and with such a feeling of regret that things were as they were, that she was saved from feeling a fool.

She picked up the third volume of the *Voyages* and began reading aloud the journeys of John Chilton of London in New Spain and the provinces of California. And her father lay back on his pillows, stroking her puppy absently with one hand, and gave himself up to their travels.

Yet part of his mind must have stayed behind in High Ashfield for, after a page or two, he broke in upon her reading.

"You must miss Ralph, Kate."

"Yes . . . yes, I do."

She paused for a moment, contemplating her loss.

"I miss him very much."

And then, since there was nothing more to be said—and nothing more was asked—she went back to her reading.

But a moment later, he broke in again.

"But you've a good friend in little Tamsin Pascoe, so your mother says."

Tamsin *little?*

"Tamsin isn't exactly little, Father," she frowned. "She's fifteen . . . and she's quite as tall as Priscilla."

"As old and as tall as that?" he asked, smiling to himself. "Well now, lay aside the book and tell me all about her."

The burden of her secret weighed heavy on her heart. Tell him *all?* Tell him that Tamsin and Adam had sat all night on Sir Matthew Paycocke's tomb in each other's arms?

"I d-don't know where to b-begin," she stammered, looking anywhere but up into his face.

He waited patiently for her to collect herself.

"Well, she must be a very kind friend to have given you this puppy," he said at last, trying to help her along.

"Sh-she is. She is. T-Tamsin's very kind."

What more could she say? That Tamsin was loving and tender and penniless and gay? And that Adam had plighted her his troth?

Her father lay back stroking Polly and looked at her curiously. The silence between them seemed to stretch as wide as the sea, and the storm that lay ahead was dark on the horizon.

At last, he asked quietly, "What's the matter? You don't usually stammer as badly as you're stammering now."

She searched about in her mind and stumbled upon the truth.

"I . . . I w-want you to l-like T-Tamsin, Father . . . as m-much as I do."

"Don't you think I will?" he asked, puzzled.

"Oh, I do hope you w-will, Father," she burst out, almost in tears. "Please, please, . . . always l-like Tamsin."

73

Adam

6

As the storm approached, the whole world darkened about them. Day after day the clouds poured rain; and together with the rain fell a blight of lost hope. The crops that were still unharvested rotted in the fields, sheep sickened, prices rose, spotted fever appeared in the villages around about, and in London whole families were stricken with the plague.

"The Lord chastens us, my friend," said Mr. Pratt discomfortingly when he brought them the news.

Their father was better now and received their neighbors in the house-room.

Old Mr. Liggett, who picked his way down the muddy lane to welcome home his friend, brought tidings that were even more grievous.

"There's trouble in the county, John. Trade's bad and prices too high."

"Things'll get better."

But their old guest shook his head sorrowfully, declaring that things had never got better—not in his lifetime, and that folk could not endure much more.

74

"Mark you, John, there'll be riots in Essex afore the winter's out. There's a mort o'hotheads 'll lead them on."

"Hotheads in Essex, Sam, in this weather?"

Kate, glancing up from her wool, saw that her father was gazing out of the window, half-smiling at the rain.

"Aye, John!" exclaimed Mr. Liggett, exasperated by his calm. "You've been away too long. You don't know how men grumble among themselves.

"The young folk . . . they say we've done wrong by the King . . . and by the country, too. It's *we've* brought this ruin . . . it's *our* fault they say, for taking up arms against the King."

Kate watched her father. He was now giving his friend his whole attention.

"They'll be the sprigs of the King's Party, Sam. A young Lucas, maybe, or a young Barker or a Torkenton. Of course, they'd speak so."

"No. They be our own children who speak out against us."

"Sam, not your Hezekiah?" her father asked gently.

"Aye," replied their old neighbor sourly. "And other folks' children, too."

Her father frowned in puzzled thought.

"They were too young, perhaps, to remember what the country endured from the King and his ways."

"Aye, and are now too old and too stubborn to be reminded. We're forgotten men, John. You'll find you've fought your battles in vain."

When their visitor had gone, her father looked down upon her, sitting there on the floor.

"Kate, child," he asked, smiling wryly, "was ever a man more plagued by Job's comforters?"

And Kate, looking up into his gaunt face, so wasted by illness—and knowing what new griefs still lay ahead —felt an intolerable ache, not only for her father but for the rest of them also. For, while she had sat listening to old Mr. Liggett, it had come to her in a flash of understanding that *Adam* must be one with his son Hezekiah. Adam revered the name of the fallen, King. That was why he had shaken her so cruelly at the clipping. Perhaps Adam, too, thought his father had fought his battles in vain.

Was there never to be an end to the wretchedness brought by this terrible civil war?

Ralph was the next—unlikely—bringer of bad news.

He had been sent up by his uncle from the Hythe to spend the day at High Ashfield.

"Father," he cried, bursting into the house-room. "Your old commander's dead."

"The Earl of Essex? Yes, I know."

Adam had heard the news four days ago when he was last in Colchester.

Yet Kate saw at once that it was not these tidings that brought Ralph and her father so much grief. Indeed, the honor heaped upon the great Parliament hero at his funeral was a source of pride to them both.

"They've set his effigy up in the Abbey," said Ralph excitedly. "And it's wearing the buff coat and the scarlet breeches and the white boots that he wore at Edgehill."

"I saw him, wearing them, Ralph," smiled his father proudly.

It was the quarreling among the victors, the bitter feuds between the Presbyterians and the Independents now racking London, Parliament, and the whole country that Ralph and her father found so hard to bear.

"I don't understand it, Father . . . I don't understand it at all. We were so nearly defeated at Edgehill. We so nearly lost the war. And then we defeated them at Marston Moor and at Naseby. And yet *now* . . . when the King has surrendered to the Scots . . . we're all squabbling among ourselves. What's *happened* to our cause?"

A weak ray of sunshine filtered through the rain-soaked windowpane and made strange wobbling blobs on the floor and over her father's worn army breeches.

"I don't understand, myself, Ralph," he replied sadly. "Perhaps it's much easier to fight a war than it is to patch up a peace."

Then, with an effort, he seemed to put the outside world at a distance and smiled at Ralph with affection. It was good to see him at home, he said.

Yes, home. Home. That was it! he went on. That was where their duty must lie in the coming months.

"If we keep faith with one another here at High Ashfield and with you and Ben on the *Essex Maid*, why then, you'll see, we Ryders will ride out this grievous time."

It was a poor little pun, Kate thought—as weak as the sunshine. But it was bravely said.

"And now that you're home again," he continued, more cheerfully, "and that it's stopped raining at last, I've got a job for the three of us to do."

"A job for *you?*" Kate exclaimed, looking anxiously at her father.

He had left his sickbed less than a week ago.

"For me," he assured her, smiling. "I'm neither so old nor decrepit, Kate, that I can't climb a ladder and help give St. George a new coat of paint."

And that—in spite of her mother's protests and Priscilla's silent scorn—is what the three of them did that cold and blustery September day. Ralph rummaged about at the back of the barn and found a crumbled cake of blue paint and another of white tucked behind the remains of the red, and they gave Tom Ryder's saint blue armor, a white shield with a red cross on it, and a sword dripping with red blood.

"And what about the dragon?" Ralph asked, when they had done.

77

"I've no heart for the dragon," their father replied. "We'll leave him with your scarlet tongue. That's quite good enough for him."

The storm broke a week later while the five of them were seated at supper in the house-room.

They were eating rabbit pie.

"I wonder your friend Tamsin hasn't come to see you, Kate," her father said.

"Nor yet my good neighbor, Lucy Cooper!" exclaimed their mother indignantly. "Lucy's a great one for visiting . . . and with you home, John, I'm right hurt she hasn't called."

"Her husband's come back from the army," said Adam shortly. "He returned the same day as you, Father."

"And does that stop his wife and his niece from calling upon their friends? He isn't ill, is he? Or wounded?"

Adam shook his head and looked uncomfortable.

"He's a sour sort of man, Father. I hope he isn't your friend."

He had called in at Langby once or twice in the last month, he said, and had found Mrs. Cooper and the Pascoes kept hard at their tasks and much oppressed by his coming home.

"Dan was never a sweet man," their father confessed. "And the way things are now can but sharpen his temper."

"They'll not be over at High Ashfield very often," Adam went on. "Not Mrs. Cooper . . . and . . . and . . . and Tamsin."

"Nor yet Simon, I hope," Priscilla threw in wilfully.

"Priscilla!" exclaimed their mother in surprise.

"I don't care if I never see either of the Pascoes ever again," she burst out.

"Priscilla! What's happened? The five of you were such friends."

"People can change their tastes, Mother," she replied tartly. "I've changed mine. The Pascoes are nobodies. You know they are."

"Adam? Kate? What's happened?" cried their bewildered mother.

Adam did not attempt to answer her.

Instead, he put down his knife and fork, got up from the table, and stood formally, slightly bowing his head, in front of his father.

As Kate watched him, her heart seemed to miss a beat.

In spite of the bowed head, he stood there, resolute and braced for battle. The burden he had carried all the summer had fallen from his back.

"Father," he announced. "I beg leave to marry Tamsin Pascoe."

"Adam!" cried their mother.

"No, Adam! No!" burst out Priscilla. "Not Tamsin!"

"The child has no portion, son," exclaimed her mother, bewildered. "No dowry . . . nothing!"

"Father?" asked Adam, standing firm at his post.

Their father looked up at him for a long time, first shocked and then saddened. Then he looked away and bowed his head in thought.

"Your mother is right, Adam," he replied at last. "Tamsin is but a child."

"She is fifteen."

"That is still not very old."

"Girls have married younger than that."

"And lived to rue it," burst out their mother.

"It is a rash thing . . . a sudden thing that you are proposing," continued their father. "Have you considered it well?"

"Yes."

"Have you thought what such a profitless marriage will do to us here at High Ashfield?"

"What do you mean?"

"Tamsin can bring you nothing with her," he said gently. "No painted cloth . . . no money . . . no High Meadow."

"We have enough."

Their father shook his head.

"You have forgotten your sisters, my son. Can I send them as portionless to their husbands as Tamsin must go to hers?"

"What do you mean?"

"We must give land to Priscilla's husband . . . and when the time comes, to little Kate's too."

"And we'd looked to your wife's portion, Adam,"

lashed out their mother angrily, "to make good this loss."

"You'll beggar me and Kate," Priscilla cried out bitterly. "None but poor men will take us."

Attacked from so many sides, Adam stuck out his chin.

"I love Tamsin," he rounded on them all. "I have plighted her my troth."

Kate saw that for the first time their father flushed with anger.

"Without asking our permission?" he whipped out.

"Dear Heaven, Adam!" gasped their mother. "Have you got the girl with child?"

"*No*, Mother!" he shouted, enraged. "I am no fornicator. Nor is she."

"Then your summer lust must die," she said. "Just as fast as it quickened."

"I said I *loved* Tamsin," he shouted again. "Not *lusted after* her. Does my mother not know the difference?"

"Peace, son," ordered their father sharply.

"I know that Lucy Cooper and Tamsin have caught you," swung back their mother angrily. "It was a clever trick. They looked to High Ashfield. That's it! It's a fine prize for a penniless girl."

Kate felt sick at her mother's injustice.

"Margaret!" exclaimed their father sternly. "Do you, too, keep a watch on your tongue. What you say comes not from the Lord. You know it yourself."

Lucy was a good and trusted friend, he went on forcefully. And Tamsin, too, was a good girl. A loving girl. A generous girl. She had said so herself. Kate had said it, too. And was not Adam enough of their son to choose a bride who—at least in herself—was worthy of his love?

Then he turned toward Adam.

There was a worse bar to their marriage, he said gravely, than any of those that they had yet touched on.

"What's that?" demanded Adam warily.

"Why, Tamsin and her brother are not of us. They have been brought up in the King's Party."

"What of it?"

"Can the two of you live together without bitterness, knowing always that Tamsin's father was killed in battle fighting against your own?"

"It was you who fought against Captain Pascoe, Father," Adam replied bluntly. "Not me."

"And is my cause not your cause, Adam?" he asked quietly.

A long silence fell in the house-room. A dreadful silence.

"Your cause is *not* my cause, Father," Adam said at last. "King Charles is our lawful king, ordained by God. Your armies . . ."

"Adam!" burst out their mother.

So she had been right! Kate thought aghast. It was all true. The very worst that she had feared.

"You, Adam! *You!* Our eldest son!" cried their mother, breaking down in bitter, angry sobs. "You've broken our hearts. You'll *kill* your father . . ."

"No, Mother," he replied. "I shall not kill my father. I love him too well."

And he hoped that his father loved *him*, he went on. The war was over. The King's cause had been defeated. The three of them could live here at High Ashfield in peace with one another—the issue put behind them.

"Perhaps I should not have told you," he said, troubled in himself, seeing the terrible pain he had inflicted.

Their father was gray with grief.

"I . . . I did not want you to think . . ." Adam stumbled on, "that . . . that Tamsin and I would ever quarrel over your hateful war."

Kate saw that her father was staring at the cold rabbit pie, looking utterly undone.

Then he stirred himself.

"What makes you think that our war is over?" he asked Adam bleakly.

"Why, the King is your prisoner."

"And what should we do with him now?"

"God knows!" Adam replied, shrugging his shoulders in sudden contempt. "That's the affair of the Scots and your Parliament."

Their father shook his head.

"It is the King himself—and the people—who will have to decide."

"How can a prisoner decide?"

"He has but to accept very reasonable terms."

"And strut like a king in a puppet show ever after?" flashed Adam bitterly. "But King Charles *cannot* do so! He is the Lord's anointed!"

Their father stretched out his hands in despair. But that was the very reason, he said wretchedly, that he had gone away to fight all those years ago. If Englishmen were to know freedom, the King's power *had* to be curbed: Parliament, not the King, had to instruct the government of the nation.

"And you tell me that our war is ended?" he replied wearily. "The fire is not doused, Adam. It is but smoldering. It may burst into flame with the next puff of wind."

In the silence that followed, Kate could hear nothing but Polly gnawing a bone under the table.

"If it is so . . . as you say . . ." said Adam, taut with anguish, "then God help us. God help all of us here in this house."

Flight

7

"God help us. God help us all," Kate prayed over and over again in bed that night.

Her family, which was her world, was tearing itself apart.

When Priscilla at her side fell at last into a fretful sleep, she lay on, staring into the darkness, hearing her father trying to comfort her mother in the room along the passage. Then, hours later, after she had dozed, she listened again to the murmurings and knew that it was her mother who was trying to console her father.

It was a terrible thing to her—this desolation in her home.

Perhaps because of her prayer, God did, indeed, help them.

"Adam," said her father at breakfast next morning after he had said grace. "We will walk up to Langby together this morning, you and I."

"To see Mr. Cooper?" Adam asked in a quick gasp of joy.

Her father nodded.

"That is what is usual, my son, when a young man wishes to marry a young woman."

Priscilla gave a noisy sob.

"Let Adam saddle Steadfast," said her mother.

But no. Her father said that he would walk. It would do him good. Besides, Smy needed the horse for the plowing.

Since it was apple-picking time, Kate ran out with a basket as soon as the meal was over and stood halfway up a pippin tree, watching her father and her brother slowly crossing the High Meadow, both dressed in their Sunday best, her heart full of affection for them both.

"Please God put it into Mr. Cooper's mind to say 'yes'," she prayed as she reached for the next apple.

She would not ask the Almighty for another single thing—not for a whole month—if only Mr. Cooper said "yes."

Now that Adam's love for Tamsin was out in the open, the thought of their marriage was a joy to her, a happiness so shining that it blinded her to her father's fears that the war might begin again. As Adam's wife, Tamsin would come to live at High Ashfield forever and ever. She and her friend would never be parted.

She began picking the apples in a fever of childish superstition, sure that the more apples she could pick the more likely it would be that Tamsin would come to live with them. If she could pick eight basketfuls and get them stored one by one in the loft, then the matter was settled.

An hour later, as she was filling her seventh basketful, she was so certain that all would be well that she began seeing Tamsin wherever she looked: in the red-cheeked pippins, in the bright sunshine falling slant-wise on the grass, in Polly's anxious, loving eyes as she sat at the foot of the tree, mutely begging her to come down.

And then, as she climbed down the ladder from the loft, having stored her seventh basketful, she glanced across the yard and her heart fell. Something must have gone wrong. Adam and her father had returned already. There they were, disappearing through the kitchen door, a burden of lost hopes bowing their backs. Knowing that she had no right to intrude, she trailed back to the orchard, wondering what had happened and miserably fearing the worst.

She did not have to wait long to hear the truth.

Almost straightaway, Priscilla ran out of the farm-yard and into the orchard, her face bright with gladness.

"It's all off, Kate," she shouted, laughing, as she stood at the foot of the tree looking up. "Mr. Cooper won't have him!"

"Won't have who?" asked Kate, letting an apple drop out of her hand.

"Won't have Adam, of course. He says he's heard all about Adam from Mr. Liggett . . . and he won't have his niece marry with a turncoat!"

"A turncoat? Adam?"

"Don't be stupid, Kate. You heard yourself what he said last night."

"And Tamsin?" she asked, trying to swallow back her tears.

"Didn't even set eyes on the girl," shot out Priscilla triumphantly.

Mr. Cooper, she said, had packed Tamsin off to his sister at St. Osyth to be out of harm's way.

In her unhappiness, Kate gazed down unseeing into her sister's upturned face.

"Poor Adam! Poor Tamsin!" she said, the tears blurring her eyes.

"And lucky us!"

"Lucky?" she asked numbly. "How can we be lucky?"

"Why, you goose, now that their stupid marriage is called off, we'll get our rightful dowries after all. I'll get the High Meadow, perhaps. And you . . . you . . .

why, if you can get a man to marry you . . . you might get the seven-acre field."

Kate shook away her tears and, looking down, at last saw her sister, sharp and clear.

What she saw through the green leaves was fair-haired and pretty and hardhearted and mean. How terrible to balance people's happiness against a parcel of land!

In her hatred of her sister's meanness, she reached out her hand.

A moment later Priscilla screamed with pain. She rocked backward and forward, covering her face with her hands.

"Kate, you fool," she cried in a muffled voice. "One of your apples has fallen smack on my nose."

Once back in the kitchen, the two of them found their mother beside herself with rage.

"I'll Dan Cooper him," she threw at them as they set down the skep of bruised pippins. "To turn away our Adam! . . . And he a man of straw to us Ryders . . . a greasy sutler in the camp kitchens . . ."

Kate saw that tears were running down her cheeks.

"But aren't you . . . aren't you glad, Mother," blurted out Priscilla, breathing thickly through her mouth.

"Glad the fellow's insulted our son?"

Adam was a good boy, she rounded on them both. A fine son. A hard worker. And his father . . . why, he was the bravest, most noble, most respected yeoman in the whole of Essex.

"And worth a hundred and twenty good lusty acres to that moldwarp's seventy-three."

"But Adam's a Royalist," persisted Priscilla, thick in the head.

"You're a *fool*," stormed her mother. "A boy that's caught the measles isn't peagoose all his life."

Adam had not understood how it had been for them

87

all before the war. He would get over his folly now that his father was home.

"You see if he doesn't."

Kate, understanding the pain of her mother's hurt pride, longed to throw her arms around her neck and tell her that she understood.

In the wet, depressing weeks that followed, Kate wondered wretchedly whether the whole world had not caught the measles and were likely to stay peagoose to the end of time.

It rained so hard that neither the oats nor the wheat could be sown; and the roads were so deep in mud that she and Priscilla and her mother were imprisoned in the steading. Adam, now bitter and withdrawn, trudged off for hours into the rain—no one knew whither. And their father, his face taut and pale, went about his work in stable, barn, and yard with a sad, tight courage that nearly broke Kate's heart.

Once a week he rode into Colchester to sell the yarn that the three of them were spinning—and brought back the news.

The kingdom, he told them, seemed poised on the brink of ruin. Many thousands of soldiers, like himself, had returned to their homes penniless, owed months— and even years—of pay by the Army. And what had they found? Farms neglected, prices high, and the Parliament taxes so grinding that trade had been almost brought to a standstill.

"It is all true what Sam Liggett told me," he said gravely one night as the three of them were busy with the wool. "Adam is not alone in longing for the King's return."

Kate wondered how they all managed to go on milking and spinning and cooking and eating—just as at other times; why the cocks still crowed and the hens still laid eggs in so much grief.

She longed for her brother Ralph.

As the long, dreary autumn dragged by, she wondered about Adam and grew sadder still. Where did he go each day, tramping out into the rain by himself? Not to Tamsin. That was certain. There was no gleam of hope in his shut-away face when he returned—no hint of some secret, stored-up joy.

And then, as October passed and November came, she grew angry with her brother.

Why had he not gone over to St. Osyth weeks ago and seized his bride by force—set her free from her uncle's unkindness—and brought her home to them all? That was what one of King Arthur's knights would have done. In her disappointment, she grew angrier with him still. Perhaps, she thought bitterly, her mother had been right after all. Perhaps it had been lust that he had felt for Tamsin in the summer, not love—something as shallow and unworthy as Simon's brief lust for Priscilla.

Then, in the middle of December, the frosts came.

The sun shone by day; at night the moon gazed down on a hard and sparkling world. Dawns and sunsets flamed with a splendor that even Bet could not remember before.

And Adam came slowly back to himself.

He looked keener, brighter, more resolute. He was gentler with his mother, more attentive to his father.

"Father," he said one evening, after they had been discussing their plan of plowing up the High Meadow, "there is so much work to be done on the farm, would it not be better that you should hire one of the soldiers returned from the war to . . . to help us here at High Ashfield?"

Her father raised his head from mending a saddle and looked across at him for a strangely long time.

Then he nodded his head.

"What you say is thoughtful and wise, my son," he said sadly. "I will see to it."

Then, two days before that first doleful Puritan Christmas, Adam came to his father and asked for the loan of old Steadfast. He would be gone all day, he said.

Kate watched him ride away up the lane, the glow of the sunrise bathing horse and rider and hedge and lane in a strange radiance of red light.

In midafternoon, while the three of them were at their carding and spinning and her father was reading aloud to them to lighten their task, there came a great clatter in the farmyard and the loud snorting of a hard-ridden horse, followed by a thundering knock on the kitchen door. She ran to open it, and a thin, pale-faced, angry man she had never seen before pushed roughly past her and strode straight through the kitchen into the house-room.

"She's gone, Ryder!" Dan Cooper shouted at her father, shaking his fist. "My niece—and your son!"

"Tamsin and Adam!" exclaimed her mother, knocking over her spinning wheel as she jumped to her feet.

"Aye, woman, the pair on 'em!" he roared. "An' I'll have the flarneckin' maukin back afore your lad's smotched her."

"Dan Cooper!" Her mother faced the intruder, beside herself with indignation. "Our son . . . he's no . . ."

"Peace, Margaret," said her father sharply. "And peace, too, neighbor. You speak evil."

"Evil words for evil deeds, Ryder. Your son . . . he's stolen the strumpet."

"Tamsin's no strumpet!" exploded her mother.

"Dan," whipped out her father in cutting anger, "the Devil speaks in you. Not the Lord."

"Devil or Lord—Lord or Devil," bellowed Tamsin's uncle, "I'm takin' the wanton mawther back home with me."

"Home with you?" exclaimed Kate's bewildered mother.

"You heard, woman. Go, fetch her down."

"But they're not here."

"Then where are they?" Dan Cooper roared.

"Gone to a minister, I trust, to get married," said her father.

"Married?"

Her father, who had risen from his chair long ago, now fixed their neighbor with blazing eyes.

Adam had come humbly and honestly to Langby, he told him. They had both come. Father and son. They had offered Tamsin marriage and a good home and had asked nothing in return. It was he, Dan Cooper, who had turned them away. Turned them away, reviling and heaping bitter scorn on the boy. If the young people had now taken matters into their own hands, then it was disobedient of them—but not downright wicked. The wickedness, her father told him sternly, lay in the violence within his own heart.

Mr. Cooper snorted furiously.

If the pair of them were not here, he shouted, then he'd be off scouring the countryside looking for them. And if he did not find them and Adam failed to marry the girl—then he'd have the law on him.

"And on you, too, Ryder," he yelled back from the kitchen as he strode out to his horse.

"Where can they be, John?" whispered her mother, when it was almost dark. "They have nowhere to go but here."

Their father shook his head.

Shivering at her mother's words, Kate saw in her mind the vast sweep of the Essex countryside laid out flat as the sea: bare hedges, fields, meres—all frozen and sparkling in the moonlight—and with nowhere for Adam and Tamsin to go.

Night came and Mr. Cooper did not return.

Had he found them, they all wondered. Was Tamsin back at Langby in tears? Was Adam wandering about alone, too distraught to ride home?

Not knowing what to think, they went comfortless to bed, leaving the kitchen door unlocked so that the two of them could creep in quietly out of the cold.

Kate lay awake for hours, straining her ears for the first hint of their return, for the distant ringing of Steadfast's hoofs on the iron ground. But no sound came. The silence was as cruel as the frost. Nodding at last, though shivering with cold, she pulled Polly under the bedclothes to make her warm.

And then, suddenly, she was wide awake. She lay stiff, without moving, trying to think what it was that she had heard. Whatever noise had woken her had woken Polly, too. The puppy had pushed up her muzzle and was growling softly into her ear.

Then it came again.

The soft munching sound of a horse with his feed . . . and the furtive muffled footfalls of someone moving about on straw.

They are home! she thought joyfully, gathering up the puppy and slipping cautiously out of bed. They are seeing to Steadfast in the stable.

She crept down the stairs and in the warm kitchen picked up her father's worn buff coat and flung it over her shoulders; then she slipped her bare feet into her mother's clogs and let herself out into the yard.

She came upon Adam in the darkness of the stable in the act of throwing a horse blanket over Steadfast's back.

"Adam!" she whispered.

"Kate!" he exclaimed, spinning around on his heel.

"Where's Tamsin?" she asked, peering into the deeper darkness.

"Safe."

"Not here?"

He shook his head.

"Where then? Mr. Cooper didn't find you?" she asked in sudden panic.

He shook his head again; and Kate, getting used to the darkness in the stable, sensed that he was smiling.

"She is safe with friends," he whispered.

"And . . . and you are married?" she burst out in excitement.

"Tomorrow we shall be wed."

She flung her arms around him and kissed him.

"Then come into them, Adam," she said joyfully. "They'll be so pleased . . . so happy."

But Adam, to her surprise, clapped his hand over her mouth.

"No," he whispered hoarsely. "I've brought Steadfast back. And now I'm off."

"But Adam," she urged desperately, her voice muffled by his hand, "you can't. You *can't!*"

He let her go at last.

"They've been so unhappy for you both," she whispered. "Mr. Cooper . . . he . . . he said dreadful things."

Her brother stood close to her in the darkness.

"It's better so, Kate," he whispered. "Tell them . . . tell them we're safe . . . and that we'll be married before noon . . . and . . . and that I crave their forgiveness."

"But you can ask them for that yourself," she hissed back.

He looked down at her and slowly shook his head.

"Aren't you coming home, both of you, after you've been married?" she asked, feeling hollow with disappointment.

No. They were not coming back to High Ashfield, he replied gently. He had thought it all out. It was better not.

"But why? *Why?*"

He stood looking down at her for a long time without speaking.

"Because Father was right," he said at last. "The war is not over. We shall be fighting again within the year."

She burst into tears.

He held her close to him.

"Is it not better, Kate," he said sadly, "that father and son should not fight against each other, here at High Ashfield?"

Her grief rolled over her like a huge breaker in the sea.

"But how'll you both live?" she sobbed.

"I've found employment," he whispered. "We have friends."

It was humble work, he confessed. But it would suffice.

"But where'll you find l-lodging?"

They had been lent a room, he told her. He had not been idle in the weeks since Mr. Cooper had refused him and banished Tamsin to St. Osyth.

Then he kissed her gently and was off.

"Go in quickly, Kate," he threw back at her as he strode out of the stable door. "You're as cold as a fish."

That cold, winter dawn, her mother was beside herself at what Kate had to tell her.

"To leave us without a word!" she cried, distraught. "Adam . . . our son, whom we love! To slink off from us like . . . like a thief in the night!"

And once again, she rounded upon Kate for not having woken them up.

"How *could* you have let him go?" she stormed.

"School yourself, Margaret," said her father gently, taking her mother aside. "Would you not have railed at your son last night as you are now railing at this child?"

Was it not better, he went on quickly, that Adam had left them in the way that he had chosen for himself?

"Without our blessing?" her mother cried.

"He knows that he takes that with him."

However grievously he had hurt them, he said, Adam had behaved like an honest man. He had declared himself openly. He had taken nothing from them. Indeed, throughout his young life he had given them of his best.

"Of his best?" flared her mother. "Is it 'of his best' that he goes against his own father and joins himself with our enemies?"

"He has been a good steward, Margaret. A good steward to High Ashfield."

95

He had only to see the state of his neighbors' farms, he explained, to realize how hard Adam must have worked.

"Of course he worked hard, Father," burst out Priscilla, hoarse with indignation. "It's *he* who's to inherit the farm!"

Kate blushed guiltily, knowing that she had once thought the same thing.

Their father looked at them sadly, but showed no surprise.

"And you, my daughters," he said quietly. "You, too, have worked hard. We have both been much blessed in our children."

After prayers that early morning, her father laid aside his Bible and told them humbly that he acknowledged his debt to them all.

"Your *debt*, Father?" Kate exclaimed, bewildered.

"Yes, Kate, my debt."

A debt, he went on, that he would now set himself to repay. It was now *his* turn to take on the stewardship of High Ashfield. He would repay his debt to Adam by keeping his inheritance in good heart through the troubled time that was to come. He would repay his debt to Ralph—perhaps by setting him up with a cargo . . .

"And your debt to me, Father?" broke in Priscilla, insistently.

Kate and her mother gasped.

But her father merely smiled, a strangely cheerful, almost mischievous smile.

"To you, my daughter, I will repay my debt by finding you a good husband."

Between the Wars

8

As she went about her tasks in the yard on that frosty Christmas Eve, Kate saw that her father had set himself to give Adam and Ralph and Priscilla something tangible that each of them wanted—something that he could achieve by his own hard work.

But he had not mentioned Kate. What did *she* want? What could he do for *her?* And, with her hands and feet growing numb in the frosty air as she cleaned out the hen house and brought fresh straw from the barn, she told herself sadly that he could do nothing. He could not give her a pretty face. He could not set her free from this thralldom by turning her into a boy. He could not even give her contentment of mind. He could do nothing. Nothing at all. She loved and honored him, but he could not alter the lowly estate to which God had called her. And it was not only a lowly estate, but a lonely one also. Ralph had left her. Adam had gone. Tamsin had gone. And soon Priscilla would be off to her husband. What could her father do to turn back such events?

Early in the New Year the three of them had spun enough yarn to pay the clothier for her father's new coat.

"Now, Priscilla," said her mother, "we'll begin spinning for *you*."

"For me?"

Why, she asked briskly, were there not sheets and a dress to buy against her wedding?

"No daughter leaves your father's roof . . . not without a pair of hempen sheets and a pair of linen ones . . . and more if we can make it so."

"But, Mother, I haven't got a suitor yet!" Priscilla pouted.

"Your father'll be off scouring the country soon as the ways are clear."

It was best to have everything prepared, she said; so they must work hard—all three of them.

And work hard they did, carding and spinning long into the dark evenings, Kate resigning herself to the tedium with as good a grace as she could muster and banishing from her mind the books on the parlor shelf.

No word came from Adam or Tamsin beyond Adam's brief note that they were married. No Ralph came whistling up from the jetty. No Mrs. Cooper came walking down the lane from Langby. It was as though the family had committed some crime, Kate thought churlishly, and were shut up here at High Ashfield, condemned to the spinning.

For all her father's loving kindness, it was a dreary, weary, stay-at-home time.

Then, suddenly, on a fine spring day, the troubles of the nation burst into their quiet lives.

General Thomas Fairfax's army had come into Essex. His soldiers, they knew, were quartered on many of the farms around about them.

One morning, while her father was away in Colchester, Kate saw a party of troopers come thudding down their lane and ran into the kitchen to tell her mother, Polly barking hopefully at her heels.

"A dozen of them," sighed her mother, viewing their approach through the house-room window. "A dozen mouths to feed and a dozen horses to eat up our grass!"

Priscilla pushed close to the window to peer at them, too.

But, to Kate's surprise, her mother shoved her sharply back out of sight.

"No!" she exclaimed sharply. "They'll get bread and cheese . . . and drink up our ale, I haven't a doubt. But they'll not set their eyes on *you*, daughter. You'll not show your face out of the house . . . not all the time they're here. Do you understand? Hold the puppy. And Kate, you and I'll go and see what they want."

When the two of them came out into the farmyard, one of the troopers had already dismounted and was clubbing a hen.

"Stop it!" shouted her mother, enraged.

The man grinned back at her and began plucking the feathers out of the twitching corpse.

"Go and fetch the man of the place," ordered the young lieutenant, carelessly throwing his command at them over his shoulder as he dismounted and strode off to inspect the barn.

"Where's your authority, young man?" demanded her mother of the insolent back. "I know the rules of quartering . . ."

But the young officer—scarcely older than Adam—shrugged his shoulders and walked on.

Her mother pushed her way through the dismounting troopers and caught him by the arm. She had been the man of the place, she told him roundly, when he had been a scrubbed 'prentice boy being beaten by his master. She'd been the man of the place through four long years, while her husband—a better man than he'd

ever be—was away fighting for Parliament at Edgehill and Marston Moor.

"Show me your commission," she demanded.

Kate, close at her side, heard the troopers laughing behind them.

The lieutenant sulkily pulled out his papers.

"Very well," she said, pursing up her lips as she read the order. "I'll oblige your Major Desborough with grass for your horses and such meat and bread for your men as we eat ourselves. No more. No less. And I'll expect a ticket from your commissary. No more killing of our poultry, do you understand?"

It was bravely said.

Kate was proud of such a mother.

But what good did it do?

The men led their horses through the gate and picketed them in the home meadow and then returned; laughing in their faces, the men killed four cockerels and three pullets, hacked down the garden fence, lit a fire, and sat grilling their loved poultry on the end of the farm pitchforks.

"Come in, child," said her mother, pulling her back into the house and slamming the door.

Kate's orderly world had taken a terrible knock. As the three of them sat spinning defiantly on in silence, she tried to pick up the bits. Law, justice, and *her own mother* had been flouted by her father's army—the army that had gone to war to bring justice back to England! Was this the way of men? Was this the way the world treated women? In the bitterness of their imprisonment on that long spring day, she saw that her books had cheated her. Malory had been wrong. There was no chivalry. No inborn respect between a young man and an old woman. All that mattered was brute strength.

Something almost as bad was to follow.

At milking time, old Bet came into them with news that most of the troopers were fast asleep on top of the haystack; the rest were quietly grooming their horses in the meadow.

"Yew comin' to the milkin' mawther?" she asked, turning to Priscilla.

"No," snapped her mother.

Priscilla was to bide indoors at her side so long as those devils remained on the farm.

Then old Bet turned to Kate.

"They'll not trouble an ole woman," she grinned toothlessly. "Nor yet a little ranny like yew."

So she looked like a shrewmouse, Kate thought as she ran to the dairy for a bucket, Polly scampering at her heels.

"No, not her, Kate," said the old servant, jerking her head at the puppy. "She do so fidget poor Daisy."

Once out in the yard, Kate saw that it was as Bet had said. Eight troopers were fast asleep in the sun on top of the stack. She could see the heels of their boots.

They settled to their milking, sitting on their stools in the dark barn.

"Yew bide where yew be," said the old woman when she had filled her two pails. "I'll take these to the dairy and be back in a mite."

It was when Kate was alone that it happened.

With her head pressed hard into the flank of the cow and her fingers struggling with the udder, she suddenly smelled onions.

Onions and fried chicken.

He was there, standing over her.

"Got you!" he laughed, scooping her up into his arms.

"The milk!" she shouted.

"Damn the milk!" mumbled the trooper as he pressed his wet lips upon her mouth.

"Stop it! Stop it!" she cried out, struggling and then kicking him hard with her clog.

And then she was down in the milk and the straw, looking up into the belly of the cow—and the trooper was lying by the manger, cursing with pain.

She scrambled to her feet and fled out under the cows . . . out . . . out into the yard . . . straight into the arms of her father, just returned from Colchester.

"Father," she sobbed. "I've . . . I've broken his leg. I've . . . I've spilt all the milk."

Yes, life was a matter of brute force, she thought soberly as she lay in bed that night. Thank God she could now kick hard enough to make a man curse with pain!

Next morning the troopers rode back up the lane to the main road and left High Ashfield in peace. Her father took the new hired man up to Smy, plowing the High Meadow; and her mother and Priscilla and herself and old Bet returned to their women's work.

With still no word from Adam or Tamsin, her mother was torn with anxiety for them both.

"He said he had work, Kate?" she asked her again and again. "You are sure that he said he had work?"

"Yes, Mother," she reassured her, understanding her fear. "And friends, too, so he said."

"But where can they be?"

Where, indeed? It was as though the green fields of Essex had swallowed them up.

"Don't yew be afeard," old Bet tried to comfort them all. "They'll be lyin' up some steadin', snug over in

Suffolk. Young Adam, he can earn his bread threshing. And the mawther—why she's a tidy hand with her butter. They'll not starve."

But for them both to be working on other folks' farms! It was a bitter thought.

Still, there was Priscilla and her sheets to occupy their minds.

"Your father'll be off visiting his friends now the hired man's understood his work," her mother said. "He'll bring you back a husband."

And off he rode—once or twice a week—from Easter to Whitsun and from Whitsun on to haytime, not shirking his duty to choose well.

And then one evening, early in June, he rode home from Colchester with a smile on his face, retired into the parlor with their mother for an hour or more, and then came out to them both in the house-room.

"We've found you a husband, daughter," he announced. "John Housagoe, a young yeoman from over the border near Hadleigh."

He was a good man, he told her, and a brave one, too. He had seen how bravely he had fought at Naseby.

"How . . . how old is he, Father?" Priscilla asked, her voice trembling.

"Thirty."

Her face fell.

"You're a fool, child," said her mother sharply. "He's got his own steading . . . and sixty good acres of land."

"And he needs a wife," said her father gently. "He needs a good wife, Priscilla, in a hurry."

His wife had died three months ago, he explained, leaving him with a child.

"A widower! With a baby!"

"You can be thankful there's only one," said her mother bluntly. "And that a girl. She's not a baby. She's five years old."

"When does he come?"

"Tomorrow."

"But what if I don't like him?" she asked in panic.

Her father smiled to reassure her.

"Why then, young John Housagoe rides home to Hadleigh in the morning and looks elsewhere."

But she *did* like him.

And Kate liked him, too.

He was grave and gentle. He was also frank—and bore himself with the kind of quiet gentleness that Kate thought Ralph might one day achieve should he ever be seasoned in battle and become acquainted with grief.

"I think Father's very clever and Priscilla's very lucky," Ralph blurted out to her after he had met him.

Watching her sister through the short weeks of their courtship, Kate thought that it was something more than cleverness and good luck. She was watching a miracle. Priscilla grew gentle and charming and at peace with them all. She blossomed in love.

Goodness, Kate thought, awed by the change. Perhaps she won't be so dreadful to be married to after all.

They were married at Michaelmas—by Mr. Pratt—without pomp or festivity, in accordance with their faith and the harshness of the times, and set off for Hadleigh that same afternoon in John Housagoe's cart, together with six hempen and two linen sheets and the title deeds to the twenty-acre field.

"It will be your turn, Kate, one of these days," said her father quietly one evening when they were alone together in the house-room.

She had carded some wool and was now taking her turn at the spinning.

"To marry?" She shook her head. "I'll not marry, Father," she told him off-handedly. "I'll stay with you here."

He looked at her quietly for a long time, while she pressed the treadle and the spinning wheel whirred.

"You are too young at thirteen, my child," he said at last. "But the time will come . . . when you are eighteen . . . nineteen."

She shook her head again and turned her face away.

"Kate?" he asked sharply. "What is it? Of course you must marry!"

Her lip trembled.

"I am not pretty, Father . . . as Priscilla is pretty . . . as Tamsin is pretty."

"No. But then, you are not as old."

"Do you mean that prettiness might suddenly come to me?" she asked, never having thought of such a hope.

"It might."

"Or it might not?"

It was dark in the house-room, for it was a late autumn evening and the clouds were low. Her father continued to look at her thoughtfully out of the shadows and then rose, lit a taper, and came over to where she was.

"Well, let me look at my ugly little daughter," he said, smiling with amusement as the glow from the light warmed her cheek. "Why, she's got good eyes, a sensible mouth, a firm chin . . . It's only the nose, Kate . . . it's a little on the sosh . . . like my brother Ben's."

She wanted to throw her arms around his neck.

"Is that all that's wrong?" she asked.

She liked Uncle Ben's crooked nose. It gave him a wise, humorous look.

"That's all. You've got a *good* face, Kate—honest, intelligent, alive."

If a young man in five years' time should come looking for a wife, he told her, a lively, loving wife—not a fool—then hers was the face for him.

Speechless with joy, she whizzed the spinning wheel so fast that she snapped the yarn.

In the months and years that followed, her father's words glowed and blossomed in her heart—like fir cones thrown into a fire.

It was strange in this dark winter of 1647—just when the family at High Ashfield had dwindled to herself and her parents and she had begun to find companionship in their company and a little hope for herself—that Tamsin and, indeed, Adam, too, should have come back into her life.

Very late in December, Tamsin's Aunt Lucy came picking her way down their muddy lane.

"Margaret, here's our old friend come to see us at last," said her father, throwing open the house-room door and showing her in.

"Lucy!" cried her mother, jumping up and embracing her.

"Margaret," she burst out. "Sam's seen them . . . in Colchester. He saw Tamsin."

"How is she?" Kate broke in. "How is she, Mrs. Cooper?"

Tamsin's aunt sat down on a stool and burst into tears.

"She's with child, Margaret. She's big with child."

"Where are they living?" her father asked.

Mrs. Cooper shook her head. She did not know, she sobbed. Sam had asked Tamsin but she would not tell him.

"Was she looking well—happy? Does she thrive?" asked her mother.

Mrs. Cooper shook her head and wept afresh. Sam had said that she had looked right whittery and half-starved.

Tamsin's plight brought a silence to the room.

"Where was it that he met her?" asked her father at last. "In what street?"

"Corner of High Street with St. Helen's Lane."

"Kate, child," said her father, turning to her quickly. "Get a basket and fill it with butter . . . eggs . . . and . . . and that hand of pork. You and I will take the cart into Colchester and find them out."

They began their search where Sam had met with Tamsin, at the corner of High Street and St. Helen's Lane. It was a part of the town that both of them knew well because her father, when he came into market, always left Steadfast with Joel Webster, the ostler at the George Inn, and the inn yard opened out into the lane.

"Bless yew, Mr. Ryder," the old ostler greeted him. "And yew, too, Mis'ress Kate. It's a long time since I seen yew. An' what brings yew both into town on a Monday? Is it to see your son Adam . . . ?"

"My son?" exclaimed her father. "You know where he lives?"

"Aye," replied Joel in wonder, seeing that Adam's own father was in ignorance. "Down this 'ere lane, Mr. Ryder, lodgin' with old Mrs. Noordenbos . . ."

"The Dutch weaver's wife?"

"Widow," rumbled their friend, as he hobbled out of the yard with them to show them the way. "The young couple . . . they won't come to no harm . . . not alon' wi' Missus Noordenbos . . ."

"And how long have they been lodging with the widow?"

"A week . . . maybe ten days."

They found the house. They found the old Dutch woman. And she led them up her steep stairs.

"Tamsin, child," she said, opening the garret door, " 'ere's friends to see you."

Tamsin turned from potting a tulip in the window and flung herself into Kate's arms.

"Kate . . . dear Kate," she cried, her tears and her laughter coming both together.

And then, smiling tremulously, she turned to the stranger at her side.

"Kate . . . it . . . it is your father?"

And Kate nodding, Tamsin, big with child though she was, knelt before him and begged him to forgive her.

He raised her up, looked into her pale, smiling, tearful face and kissed her.

"Bless you, my dear daughter," he said simply. "May God have you in his care."

But it was more human care that worried them both as they jogged back to High Ashfield in the empty cart.

Sam Dyer had been right. Tamsin looked half-starved; her eyes glowed deep and large in her pale face.

Besides, the garret—though clean and furnished with the bare necessities—was as cold as a tomb.

"Come home with us," Mr. Ryder had pleaded. "Both of you come home."

But Tamsin had shaken her head and replied gently that *this* was their home. Adam had found good work with a nursery gardener outside the town walls. They would prosper now. She was sure that they would prosper.

"Is there nothing we can do?" Mr. Ryder had asked.

Tamsin had smiled at him.

"Yes, sir," she had replied. "Will you grant me a favor?"

"Name it, my daughter."

"When you drive into market . . . will you . . . will you bring Kate to visit me for a few hours?"

When Mr. Ryder had willingly granted her request and had gone downstairs to talk with the Dutch widow, Tamsin had flung her arms about Kate, laughing with all her old joy.

"Kate, Kate," she had whispered into her ear. "Isn't it *wonderful* how huge I am!"

"You need not have feared, Kate," her father said,

as Steadfast turned off the main road and trotted down the lane.

"Feared?" she asked in surprise. "Feared what?"

"I like Tamsin," he replied simply. "She has slipped into my heart."

For God and King Charles

9

Yet, though Tamsin had come back into her life, Kate soon saw that it was not the same Tamsin whom she had known at Langby, not the friend who had opened her arms and taken the whole world to her heart. The new Tamsin was happy and eager for her visits, but it was not so that she could talk about her Aunt Lucy or about Kate's parents or even about Kate, herself. Simon and Ralph she never mentioned. Their old life at Langby and High Ashfield had dropped out of her mind. Only Adam and the baby meant anything to her now.

Adam and the baby. The baby and Adam.

"It's a fine town for us to have a child in," she said one day as they walked about together under the bare trees in the meadows around the Norman Castle. "There's so many green places . . . and trees for him to climb . . . and orchards. And with all these nursery gardens, Kate, there'll always be work for Adam."

Adam growing lettuces in someone else's garden, Kate thought bitterly. Adam!—who had his father's farm!

But she held her peace.

Later, they stood on the town wall near the Balkon.

"And look where the three of us can wander on a Sunday," exclaimed Tamsin happily, sweeping her arm across the horizon to take in the wide expanse of Lexden Heath. "Just look at it all!"

Kate nodded her head and smiled. But the smile inside her mind was sadly wry.

This new Tamsin had more in common with the new Priscilla than with herself. Tamsin had, somehow, gone on ahead and shut herself up in a narrow room—at the top of a tall tower—and she, Kate, could not climb up to her.

Adam, too, had changed.

He looked taut and worn by the poverty that they must have endured in the past year. But he also looked happier, more resolute, more certain of himself.

"Kate, I'm glad you can come to Tamsin now and then," he told her frankly. "She's lonely on her own all day, especially now her time is near."

It was not unkindly said; yet his words and his manner told her plainly that he no longer knew her as Kate, his sister—the child he had carried on his shoulders on Bartholomew's Eve, the girl he had kissed good-bye in the stable in the dark—but only as Kate, his wife's friend, who could amuse her in her boredom.

It brought a chill to her heart. They had both cut themselves off from her.

A terrible thought came to her as she jogged home in the cart.

Would Ralph, when he came to marry, cut himself off from her, too?

All the winter and early spring of 1648 Kate saw how hard the menfolk worked at the plowing and how healthy and forward all looked on the farm. Yet she saw, too, that her father took no joy in his success. He was fraught with care. Long furrows creased up his brow.

"It is the times, Kate," said her mother in wretchedness. "It is, indeed, as though your poor father has fought his battles in vain."

The King, Kate knew, was now imprisoned at Carisbrook Castle in the Isle of Wight. She knew also that many of his subjects, groaning under the heavy Parliament taxes and the cruel plunderings of the unpaid army—and in despair that his captors would ever cease from quarreling among themselves—were turning with a wild hope to King Charles to put all right. There were rumblings of revolt against Parliament in Scotland and Ireland. And then, on March 23, came open insurrection at Pembroke in Wales.

Still, Scotland and Ireland and Wales were a long way off, she thought, as she went about her work. The new war, should it come, would surely not trouble them here in Essex?

And then, without warning, the troubles of the times were suddenly in their midst.

"They're talking of getting up a petition here in Essex, Kate," her father told her one day as they were driving back from Colchester.

"What sort of petition?"

"To ask Parliament to satisfy the King and to disband the Army."

She thought of the heavy taxes he had to pay and of what they had suffered at High Ashfield at the hands of the Army.

"Will you sign it?" she asked at last.

"And have it all to do again?" he burst out.

"You mean . . . ?"

"The King has learned nothing from the late war. *Nothing*, Kate. If he came back to his former power—as your brother would have him do—then your generation would have to fight for the rights of Englishmen all over again. All over again, Kate."

She saw how weary and angry he was at the hopelessness of it all and how broken in spirit that his elder son should side with the King.

Her mother was anguished, too, when she heard of the petition. She was anguished for the nation—for the farm, for her husband, for her son. But Kate saw, also, that being a woman, her mother had found a woman's gleam of hope in the darkness of the times.

"She'll be a pretty baby," she murmured one evening, looking up from sewing her grandchild's dress. "A pretty little thing . . . what with her mother's looks."

"But it's to be a boy, Mother," Kate told her gently. "That's what Tamsin says. And he's to look like Adam."

And from her mother's wistful smile as she returned to her sewing, she guessed that Tamsin, at least, was now forgiven.

Tamsin was right. It was a boy.

Two days after his birth, Kate and her father and mother drove into Colchester to bestow their blessing and their gifts on the child.

"He's a fine boy, Tamsin, a lusty boy," her mother whispered in wonder as she held her grandson in her arms.

How strange it was, flashed through Kate's mind, that she should be so gentle with this little bundle—when she had never been gentle with *them*.

"And now you have an heir for High Ashfield, son," said her father quietly to Adam, "just as I have mine."

It was a bond between them, Kate thought. The only bond at this dreadful time.

"Thank you, my daughter," said her father, turning affectionately to Tamsin, lying pale and content on her pillows. "Bless you for bringing an old man this joy."

And then the three of them were out and away from the quiet garret and back in the bitter uproar in the nation. They were clattering down East Hill where men were shouting the news.

"There's a riot in Norwich, Goodman Ryder," bawled an acquaintance in the crowd.

"A riot? What about?" asked her father, reining Steadfast in.

"It's along of their mayor being a King's man. The soldiers tried to arrest him to take him to London."

The coming war was getting nearer and nearer,

Kate thought on the way home, as she sat looking over the tail of the cart at the walls of Colchester slowly receding in the evening haze.

On May 4, a procession of two thousand Essex men, some riding and some going on foot, took their petition to the House of Commons.

When she heard the news, Kate wondered whether Adam had thrown away his hoe and had walked to London with them, and then, glancing up and seeing the deep worry in her father's eyes, she tried to find something to comfort him.

"They are only two thousand, Father," she said. "Only two thousand out of the whole county."

"Aye, Kate," came his somber reply. "But they carry the wishes of some thirty thousand more."

Then, eight days later, riots broke out at Bury St. Edmunds, scarcely thirty miles away over the Suffolk border. There was trouble, too, across the Thames River in Kent.

And then, on May 18, came her birthday. She was fourteen years old.

Next day was a Friday, and seeing the red sail of the hoy in the river, she ran down to the jetty, as was her wont, to shout a greeting to Ralph.

Then, as the *Essex Maid* approached, she saw that her uncle intended to draw alongside. Abe was standing ready to grasp the end of the jetty.

Ralph is bringing me a present for my birthday, shot through her mind.

Then Ralph appeared on deck, and she saw at a glance that her brother was carrying too heavy a burden in his mind to have remembered a birthday present.

He leaped ashore. The hoy sailed on. And they began walking up toward the farm, side by side.

"What's the matter?" she asked, glancing anxiously at his unhappy face.

"I'm . . . I'm all at sea," he burst out. "I . . . I don't understand. Kate, where's Father?"

"In the barn, I think, mending the hay rakes."

He must go to him at once, he said. His uncle had given him a terrible thrashing and had set him ashore to go up to his father and tell him what he had done.

"And what *have* you done?" she gasped. "Was it something so dreadful?"

"I didn't think it was so dreadful, not at the time," he said wretchedly. "It . . . it seemed the right thing to do . . . when . . . when I stood there . . . with the brick in my hand."

"With . . . a *brick!*" Kate exclaimed in astonishment.

Then she held her peace—for she knew what had happened. She saw it all.

Two days ago news had come to Colchester that the men of Surrey, following the example of the men of Essex, had taken a petition to Whitehall and had marched through the City shouting "For God and King Charles." On receiving no answer to their plea from the House of Commons, they had stormed into Westminster Hall. Major Briscoe at the head of five hundred disciplined Parliament soldiers had cleared the Hall of rioters an hour later with push of pike, killing eight and wounding many.

The two of them found their parents in the kitchen —where Ralph finished the tale.

"And . . . and then they fled to the boats on the river, Father . . . and the soldiers *shot* them."

"They were lawbreakers, Ralph," said their mother. "They deserved what they got."

"But they were *petitioners,* Mother . . . they were not armed. They had nothing to fight back with . . . except brickbats and lumps of coal . . . ."

"And you picked up a brick and joined in?" flashed their mother.

Ralph nodded.

Kate saw the pain in her father's face.

"My son," he said slowly, "did you think their cause was just?"

"No, Father," came the clear reply. "But they are *Englishmen*. The Commons should not have treated them so. They should have received their petition."

Kate saw the shadow pass from her father's brow.

God help them all, he replied with the saddest of smiles. They lived in dreadful times . . . times in which private justice and the public good had long been at odds . . . times in which men turned too quickly to violence to achieve their ends . . . good men as well as bad.

"Your uncle has beaten you, Ralph. I will not chide you further. It is no time for a father to be chiding a son."

When they had give him food and had brought him on his way to the top of the lane, the three of them bade him a heartfelt good-bye.

"Ralph," said their father, on parting. "In a month . . . or even a week . . . we may all be at open war again. You may well be cut off from us here at High Ashfield. You may have to decide for yourself what is best for the public good . . ."

"I'll never take Adam's choice, if that's what you mean," Ralph replied with spirit. And then added in anguish, "But I wish to God we could live in peace!"

"Amen," said their father. "So do I and your mother and Kate here. And Tamsin . . . and her babe, no doubt."

They watched him walking away down the main road to the Hythe, still moving stiffly from his beating but carrying—Kate thought—a lighter burden in his heart.

In the next three weeks the worst of her father's fears came to pass.

On May 24, the Royalist leaders, Edward Hales, Sir

William Waller, and George Goring, Earl of Norwich, assembled the Kentish Royalists near Rochester and marched to Blackheath, hoping that the City of London would rise in their support. Disappointed of the Londoners' help, they returned to Kent, but, in the course of the next week, were attacked by Sir Thomas Fairfax and were so hard-pressed by his strong and disciplined army that they returned to Blackheath.

Two days later, her father returned at the gallop from Colchester.

"The Lord help us!" he exclaimed, throwing Kate the reins. "The King's men are across the Thames!"

Lord Goring and about six hundred of his followers had crossed the river at Greenwich in boats. They had swum their horses across. They had landed in the Isle of Dogs and were now quartered at Bow and Stratford, where the London apprentices and the men of Kent were marching out to join them.

"The Royalists here in Essex—Sir Charles Lucas and the rest—they'll be joining them, too," he added as he strode into the kitchen.

When she had unsaddled Steadfast and given him his hay and returned to the kitchen, Kate heard her parents talking together in the house-room.

"Margaret, dear Margaret, it's time I put myself under Colonel Cooke's command. You know it yourself."

She heard her mother give a little cry.

"You're too old, John," she said brokenly. "Too old to go fighting any more."

"Old Steadfast's too old. Not his master."

"Then you'll have no mount."

Kate caught the desperate hope in her mother's voice.

"An old Captain of Dragoons can fight on foot."

Her poor mother! Her poor mother! To be left again!

She ran in to join her at the moment that her father was unhooking his musket from the parlor wall.

"Margaret . . . Kate," he said when he came back to them, holding the musket in his hand. "The very worst of griefs has come to our family. Adam and his hotheads must already be on their way to the Royalist headquarters. Should the fighting come this way, Kate, you must drive the cart into Colchester and bring Tamsin and the child back to High Ashfield . . ."

Kate nodded.

"And you, Margaret, must succor her and give her comfort."

"He is our grandson, John. She is the child's mother," she said. "How could I not succor them and give them what comfort I can?"

He was off within the hour.

He took them both in his arms and gave them his blessing.

They stood at the gate, heavy of heart, watching him striding up the lane in his old campaigning coat and his worn army breeches, his musket slung over his shoulder.

In this dreadful time, it is nothing but good-byes, Kate thought miserably as she saw him come to the corner and pass out of sight.

Then she turned to comfort her mother.

"Should the fighting come this way," they reminded each other.

But how were they to learn in which direction the Royalists were marching, remote as they were at High Ashfield?

"You must ride up to the village every day," her mother told her, "and ask Mr. Pratt. Tell him how it is with us here."

Kate saw the point. If anyone knew what was happening, it would be Mr. Pratt. He rode hither and thither and was the greatest busybody in the parish.

"They'll not move from London," he told her on
June 4 and again on June 5. "It's London they want . . .
and they're waiting for the Royalists of Hertfordshire to
join with them."

It seemed sensible to believe what he said.

Next day, however, he came riding down the lane
with grave news written in his face. He had just heard
that the County Committee had been seized at Chelmsford on the 4th by Colonel Farr, an officer of the trained
bands.

"The trained bands gone over to the King!" her
mother exclaimed incredulously. "Not Colonel Cooke
. . . not my husband! Never, Mr. Pratt. Never!"

No. Colonel Farr, it appeared, had carried only the

few and the foolish with him. The rest had put themselves under Colonel Whalley of the Standing Army.

"And Sir William Masham . . . and Mr. Ayloff are
taken prisoner?"

"The Lord has willed it," he said soberly.

But they would soon be set free, he assured them.
For Parliament had quickly passed an Ordnance of
Idemnity, forgiving the Essex insurgents if the committee
members were immediately released.

"Colonel Farr and his troublemakers . . . they'll
soon flock back to their duty."

As for the main body of the Royalist army, it was
still quartered at Stratford. There was no immediate
danger to any of them living here in the far northeast
corner of the county.

Three days later he came to them again. The Lord
be praised, he announced. Dover Castle had been
relieved and Canterbury had surrendered to the Parliament forces. Sir Thomas Fairfax was now free to pursue
and defeat the Royalists now quartered at Brentwood.

"At Brentwood!" her mother exclaimed in alarm.
"But you said they were at Stratford!"

A mere fifteen . . . twenty . . . miles into the
county, he said. And little good it would do them, for the
Essex men had responded to the Parliament Indemnity
and hundreds of them had gone home quietly to their villages. Better still, Sir Thomas Honeywood—praise God
that he had not been seized with the rest of the committee at Chelmsford—had ridden over to Manningtree
and secured the county magazine against the insurgents.

"You will soon have your husband home, my dear
Mrs. Ryder," he told her with confidence. "God's
enemies cannot fight without muskets and gunpowder."

Kate thought of one of God's enemies denied musket
and powder and prayed that he had slipped home
quietly like the cautious country folk and was now safe
back in St. Helen's Lane with Tamsin and his baby.

"Have no fear," said the old minister as he remounted his nag. "The Lord has us in his keeping—and Fairfax will do the rest."

"Come, Kate," said her mother briskly as Mr. Pratt rode out of the yard. "No more sitting about for us. We've the new wool to steep."

With only Smy and Bet and the hired man left, the two of them were a whole week behind with the work of the farm.

And so, for that vital Friday and Saturday—their fears lulled—they worked hard and long at High Ashfield, steeping the new wool, hoeing turnips, picking peas. And on Sunday they walked up to Bartholomew's Church and prayed for a husband and a son—a father and a brother—and for God's peace to come to their poor nation.

In the middle of the morning of that Monday—while Kate and her mother were on their knees in the herb garden, weeding the marjoram and thyme—the blow fell.

"Mistress Ryder," shouted old Smy as he hobbled in haste across the yard. "Mistress Ryder."

There was a man on the road, he panted, who said the Royalists were at Braintree.

"At Braintree!" exclaimed her mother, clambering to her feet. "Which way are they heading?"

The man did not know. But on Saturday afternoon they had pillaged the Earl of Warwick's house at Leighs, seized the armory, and carried off arms and ammunition of all sorts: two brass fieldpieces, muskets, pikes, body armor, match ball, and many barrels of gunpowder.

So they were armed after all, Kate thought in despair. Being armed, Adam would never slink home without a fight.

"Harness Steadfast," her mother told Smy. "Kate, you must go for Tamsin at once. Hurry. Hurry."

They threw blankets and wraps for the child into the cart. And just as Kate was washed and ready, standing waiting by Steadfast's head, her mother came out from the kitchen with bread and the remains of a rabbit pie and a pewter jug of fresh milk with a clean cheesecloth stuffed into its neck.

"Hold Polly, Mother. She'll be into the cart with me if you don't."

"God help you, Kate, and keep you safe," her mother said as she kissed her good-bye.

Then she was up in the cart and away along the lane and up toward the main road, flicking Steadfast gently with the whip—tense and excited—her mind racing ahead to Tamsin and the baby in St. Helen's Lane.

Braintree. Fifteen miles away. But that was Saturday night.

Where were they now? Where were Colonel Whalley and her father?

And then she remembered Sunday. No one traveled on a Sunday. No one fought on a Sunday. It was wicked to defile the Sabbath day. The Royalists must still be at Braintree . . . or very near.

As she left the village behind her, she wondered how long it took an army to march fifteen miles. It was eleven in the morning already. If they had set out at dawn . . . had slipped past Colonel Whalley . . . and were heading toward Colchester . . . ?

She whipped up old Steadfast.

But why should Lord Goring head for Colchester? The weavers in the town were all for the Parliament. Would not the Royalists strike north into Suffolk . . . where they had friends?

All the same, as she rattled through Wivenhoe Cross, she prayed that soldiers pulling cannon and drakes and barrels of gunpowder could not travel as fast as a girl in a cart drawn by a wornout old horse.

After joining the Harwich Road, she turned west and looked down on the river and at the vessels at anchor at the Hythe.

"I wish to God Ralph was with me," she thought.

And then she came in sight of the town, girt about by its ancient walls, and saw the towers and spires and the strong castle within.

All seemed quiet. There was scarcely a traveler on the road.

She whipped up Steadfast again, and they clattered past the houses in the outer suburb along East Street and then over the bridge and up East Hill and through the East Gate.

Inside the town, all was hubbub. The streets were thronged.

"What's happened?" she shouted to a man outside the George Inn.

"They're but five miles away," he shouted back. "The Mayor's ordered out the trained bands. All the gates are to be closed."

"Closed?" Kate gulped, and hurtled down St. Helen's Lane, threw down the reins, and scrambled up the stairs to the quiet attic.

"Tamsin," she gasped. "You must come at once . . . back with me . . . back to High Ashfield. You must come home."

"But Kate, *this* is my home."

As she spoke, they heard the measured tramp of the trained band . . . and then a cheer.

"You must come quickly. It's what Father said," Kate panted. "But quickly. Quickly, Tamsin. They are going to close the gates."

Tamsin shook her head.

"I must wait here, Kate, in our home for my husband to return."

Even while she spoke, it was too late.

The six gates of the town were already closed.

THE SIEGE OF COLCHESTER 1648

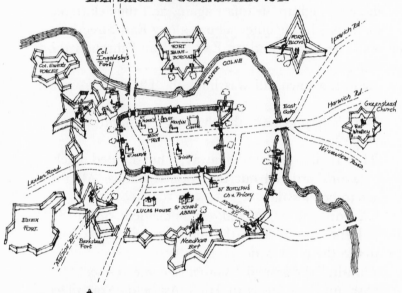

ST. JOHN'S ABBEY GATE HOUSE

The Siege

10

"We're shut in!" exclaimed Kate in panic.

Tamsin sat on in maternal calm, rocking her infant.

"It'll be all right," she crooned, as though Kate, too, was a baby.

"But it *isn't* all right!" Kate turned on her in fury.

Nothing was all right. Nothing was ever going to be all right again. Her father and her brother were at war against each other. Her mother had been left on her own at High Ashfield. Alone. Unprotected. With the Royalist army fast approaching.

"How can you say it's all right?" she flared.

In that moment she almost hated Tamsin and her obstinate calm. It was Tamsin's fault that the three of them were here; Tamsin's fault that Adam had left home; Tamsin's fault that he had gone off to fight against his father.

"Kate, don't be so cross with me," Tamsin said quietly, a slow tear rolling down her cheek. "Isn't it bad enough that Adam is in danger?"

Adam? thought Kate furiously. And what about her father? And her mother?

And then, seeing the tear, she ran to her friend in aching remorse and flung her arms around her.

This terrible war was nobody's fault—except the King's perhaps. It was certainly not Tamsin's.

"Adam and his friends'll come and take the town," said Tamsin through her tears. "And then they'll move on again. That's what they'll do."

She sounded so forlorn that Kate had not the heart to tell her that Fairfax and his Parliament army would follow swift on their heels and take the town back from them.

"When Lord Goring goes north, Kate, you'll be able to get back to your mother."

Kate nodded and prayed for the best.

Half an hour later, old Mrs. Noordenbos came up the stairs and told them that the Colchester trained band was drawn up in a very formal and warlike way across the London road, barring the Royalists' entrance to the town through Head Gate.

"Dey vill go avay, dees devils," she said stoutly. "Ven dey see vat stout 'earts ve 'ave. Dey vill march avay nord to der friends."

Tamsin flushed angrily and bent over the child.

"Your Adam ees no devil, child," said the old woman in quick compunction. "It ees war. It ees war dat makes devils of us all."

When she had left them, they both turned to the baby. And the baby—as though sensing their need for comfort—looked up vaguely at the two faces bent over him and, windily, smiled his first smile.

"Oh look, Kate!" his mother exclaimed. "Abel knows us! He's smiling!"

"Abel?"

"Yes. That's what we've decided to call him."

"Why Abel?"

"Because he's Adam's son, you goose," replied Tamsin happily. "Abel Pascoe Ryder. It's a fine name don't you think?"

Kate agreed that it was.

At four o'clock in the afternoon, Mrs. Noordenbos came to them again to tell them that Sir Charles Lucas and his troop of Essex Royalists were at that moment parleying with the captain of the trained band. Joel Webster had shouted across the lane to her that one could see them clearly from St. Mary's Church.

"Shall we go and watch them, Kate?" said Tamsin, a little ashamed of her excitement. "We might see Adam."

By the time they had reached the church and climbed up the tower, the Royalist troop had ridden away a short distance, having been refused entrance.

Kate sighed with relief. Mrs. Noordenbos had been right. Lord Goring and Sir Charles Lucas and Adam would now take themselves off out of Essex and bother Suffolk instead.

But even while she was giving the Almighty her heartfelt thanks, a weaver's apprentice, perched on a bell beam high above their heads, gave a shout.

"Look!" he cried. "Look over beyond the broom heath! Look!"

Kate strained her eyes. Afar off there was a glint of sunlight on metal and a strange, oncoming movement of the land—as though it were the sea and the tide was coming in.

"They're coming!" cried the boy. "Hundreds of them! Thousands of them!"

But *who* were coming, Kate wondered. Colonel Whalley's army and her father? The Royalists and her brother? Sir Thomas Fairfax and the main Parliament army?

She looked toward Sir Charles Lucas and his

cavaliers waiting on the London road—and her heart
sank. Even as she watched them, they began galloping off
toward the oncoming host, waving their hats.

It was the Royalists who were coming.

What could the Colchester trained band do? What
chance had a troop of weavers, tailors, millers, merchants—townsmen all—against an old campaigner like
Lord Goring at the head of four thousand men?

And what was best for the town? To be pounded to
pieces by cannon, by sakers, minions, and drakes? To be
plundered and set on fire by an angry victor?—Or to
surrender?

Sick of heart, Kate watched a short skirmish between the trained band and an advance party. And then
the gate opened and the mayor and the town officers
walked out and stood speaking with the Royalist commander.

Twenty minutes later Tamsin flung her arms
around her neck.

"Kate, they're coming in! They're coming in!
Adam'll be back home tonight."

Adam came to them in the attic three hours later,
gray with exhaustion but his eyes ablaze with excitement—an excitement so intense that he hardly showed a
flicker of surprise at finding Kate in St. Helen's Lane. It
was Charles Lucas, he said, who had persuaded Lord
Goring to come to the town; there were many Royalists
here and in the neighborhood and they hoped to pick up
recruits.

"We've fooled Colonel Whalley," he laughed.
"We've fooled the whole lot of them!"

The Royalists, he explained, had spent the night of
the 10th at Braintree and most of the 11th; but at
nightfall, knowing that Colonel Honeywood and his
Essex trained bands blocked their way at Coggeshall and
that Colonel Whalley and his army were pressing on

their rear, they had set off in a northwesterly direction toward Cambridgeshire but had then turned on their tracks, rested a space at Braintree, and then set off northeast for Halstead, slipped around Honeywood at Coggeshall, and then wheeled right and made for Colchester.

"Do you mean you've been marching all night . . . and all day!" Tasmin gasped.

"That's it," he laughed, rocking his baby absent-mindedly in his arms. "But we're days ahead of them now. They must be looking for us around Ely."

He went over and over the last few days, recounting his military adventures with a hectic abandon that appalled Kate.

It was as though he were drunk.

He had been at Leighs, he said, when they had broken into the Earl of Warwick's armory.

"You should have seen the muskets and pikes, Tamsin!" he laughed. "All piled up. Hundreds of them. And the gunpowder! That's what we lacked most."

Kate could bear it no longer. Not a word had he said about his father; his mother; herself. His old love of High Ashfield had dropped out of his mind.

Her eyes fell on the remains of the food she had brought with her.

"You'd better finish up Mother's rabbit pie," she burst out, choking with angry tears.

Then she fled down the stairs and across the lane and into the inn yard and found Steadfast.

As she stood stroking his muzzle while he munched her handful of hay, she thought of her father miles away in the darkness somewhere near Ely and her mother at home, waiting anxiously for Tamsin and herself to return, and of Ralph, belabored by Uncle Ben, wretched and torn by the violence of men's hate—and came back again angrily to Adam's cruel unconcern. War had not yet turned her brother into a devil; but it had altered him beyond bearing.

And yet, angry though she was, she knew that she, too, for one brief moment that afternoon had known the mad joyfulness of war. She had watched the Royalist army enter the town; she had seen the proud bearing of Lord Goring and Sir Charles Lucas and the other Royalist leaders as they rode through Head Gate—and the hundreds of hats tossed in the air. It had been a brave sight. And she had felt her heart throbbing with excitement.

Now, in the darkness, she shivered. Shouts of drunken revelry came to her from the inn behind.

"Eh, so yew're caught here along wi' the rest on us," said a familiar voice beside her.

It was her old friend Joel Webster.

"I don't know what to do," she blurted out.

"There's nothin' any on us *can* do, mawther, save pray to the Lord . . . and . . . and do right."

But what was right?

Well, for himself, he said, he would try to mind Steadfast and all the horses left in his charge.

"As for yew, child, yew go back up to your brother's wife. The town's no place for a slip of a girl tonight."

Everything was in confusion, he told her. Hundreds of weary soldiers were squabbling for billets.

As she turned to leave him, he called after her through the darkness, "But don't yew nor Mr. Ryder hold it agin me if they tek the horse."

"Take Steadfast?"

Their visitors were short of mounts, he explained grimly. When they moved off in a day or two, they'd take what horses they wanted.

"And anything else they've a mind to," he added. "That's war, child."

Out in the lane again, she did not at once go back to Tamsin. She was not a child. She was fourteen. With no father, no mother, no Ralph—and now, perhaps, with no Steadfast—she wanted to see for herself what she and Tamsin were likely to have to endure at the hand of war.

She found High Street and Cornhill thronged with London apprentice boys, Kentish laborers, Hertfordshire yeomen, all suddenly turned Royalist soldiers and as hollow-eyed and excited as Adam. Some were standing in doorways bullying the householder for food and lodging; others, too exhausted to fend for themselves, had given up the fight and were lying fast asleep with their backs against the walls. Picking her way over their sprawled legs, she wondered how Colchester was ever going to house—let alone feed—so great a host.

She came to the junction of Head Street with Cornhill, glanced down into the darkness at the bottom of North Hill and then crossed over and made for their old, peacetime haunt on the town wall at the Balkon. It was quiet here and deserted, save for two soldiers on guard, and quiet in the fields and the weavers' tenting grounds far below. Then she looked northwest at the night horizon in the direction of far-off Ely, and prayed for her father's safety. And as she stood there thinking of his courage and forgivingness, the memory of all that he meant to her came to her so strongly out of the darkness that she could only think that he, at that moment, must be saying a prayer for her, too.

When she returned to the attic, Adam had left. He must return to his billets, he had told Tamsin. These were in Sir John Lucas's house.

"But that's outside the town walls!" Kate exclaimed in surprise.

Yes, but it was easy to fortify, Tamsin tried to explain. It made an excellent fortress, Adam said, and protected the whole southern wall of the town from attack.

"He will come to us when he can," she told her with a tremulous smile as she put the baby back in his cradle.

And then she broke down and sobbed and sobbed.

Kate ran to her and took her in her arms.

"What is it, Tamsin?" she asked gently. "Please tell me what it is."

Adam and his friends would be off into Suffolk, she wept, as soon as they had gathered recruits and more mounts.

"I'm afraid for him, Kate. I'm terribly afraid."

Kate's fear for her father and Tamsin's fear for Adam were but young in age.

Next morning, at about noon, they were startled by a terrible clamor in the streets and a blare of trumpets along the walls.

"What's happening, Mrs. Noordenbos?" Kate shouted as she ran down the stairs to the widow.

"I do not know, child," shouted the old lady in reply. "Run and ask the ostler."

The inn yard was deserted, but looking through the arch of the inn entrance, she saw that Joel was out in the street, peering up toward Cornhill.

"What's happening, Mr. Webster?" she panted when she reached him.

"They've caught up on 'em," he shouted over the blare of the trumpets. "They're here . . . outside the walls."

"Who's here?"

"Fairfax. Whalley. Harlackenden. Cooke. The lot!"

"But they can't be," she shouted. "They're at Ely."

Another fanfare of trumpets and the frantic voice of an officer, calling his men to arms, sent her running up the hill to her old place of vantage in St. Mary's Church tower.

Her heart pounded with excitement as she saw yet again a great army drawn up outside the old town. Joel had said "Cooke." Her father must be out there with his musket—somewhere among those thousands of soldiers. And Adam was down below, outside the walls, guarding the fortress of Sir John Lucas's house. Sick with fear for them both, she watched Sir Thomas Fairfax's trumpeter and drummer approach Head Gate with a message from their general. The message must be a demand for the Royalists' surrender.

She waited there, tense and frightened and praying with all her might.

"Dear God," she urged. "Please don't let them fight. Please not. Please not. Make them lay down their arms. It's hopeless for them—you must see that for yourself. They're caught here like . . . like rats in a trap. But get Adam away . . . please God. *Please.*"

But God must have been away that noontide attending to other troubles in His tragic world—for there came a sudden shout of derision from the soldiers at the gate, and the trumpeter and drummer galloped back toward the Parliament headquarters, followed by howls of laughter from the soldiers manning the walls.

"What's happened?" she asked a townsman, as she ran back across Head Street.

The man looked grave.

"The Lord preserve us!" he replied. "They say this Earl of Norwich, this Lord Goring, he's returned the General a scurvy answer—said he'd heard General Fairfax was ill of the gout but that he'd 'soon cure him of all diseases!' "

She did not at first understand what he meant.

"By killing him?" she gasped, suddenly taking it in.

"Aye, mawther; that's what he means."

"So they'll fight? They'll not surrender?"

As he nodded his head, the man looked at her in despair.

"The Lord help us poor people of Colchester— whichever way it goes," he groaned.

She was back with Tamsin in St. Helen's Lane before General Fairfax's fury was unleashed upon the town and its unwelcome defenders.

Hearing the thunder and screams of battle, the two of them clung to each other and to Abel, appalled by the violence of the tragedy that had come upon them.

"Dear Lord," Kate begged in silent anguish. "Make it quick. Make our army overrun the walls swiftly . . . so that there's an end to it all."

But again the Lord was deaf.

The fighting was all around the Head Gate, Joel shouted up to them late in the afternoon. The besiegers had forced their way through the gate and had fought a passage halfway up the steep hill of Head Street, but they had been cut off by a Royalist force hiding in St. Mary's Churchyard and then attacked by a troop of horsemen riding down upon them from the junction of Head Street and Cornhill. Now it was hand-to-hand work. The

Royalist officers had dismounted from their horses and had seized pikes.

"It's bloody war," Joel yelled up. "Hundreds are killed."

The sound of fighting all along the southern wall of the town rolled on and on long into the night. And then, gradually, it died down.

"The Royalists must have repulsed them," Kate whispered to Tamsin in the darkness across the sleeping child.

Adam came to them at three in the morning. Kate lit a taper, and Tamsin cried out. He had a bloodstained bandage wound about his head.

But he brushed aside her grief.

"We've beaten them off," he cried, the same wild look of exultation burning in his eyes. "We've defeated the great Fairfax. We've killed scores of his rogues."

"And have you killed Father?" Kate shouted at him, enraged.

"Father!" he gasped.

"He's out there fighting," she burst out in a storm of passion. "He put himself under Colonel Cooke of the trained band more than a week ago."

"Father!" he gasped again.

She could not bear it. She fled from the attic, crossed the inn yard, and crept in again to the dark stall. She laid her face against Steadfast's muzzle and wept bitterly. There seemed no end to the agony of the times.

Then she wiped her eyes with her sleeve—and did what she knew she had to do. She walked out into the High Street, past soldiers lying sleeping against the walls of the houses, past moaning, wounded men, walked up Cornhill and crossed Head Street and came to the scene of the fighting. They had thrown the dead bodies of the besiegers down among the gravestones in the churchyard.

By the first light of day, she looked sadly into one dead face after another.

Then she went back to St. Helen's Lane.

Her father had not been there.

By full light, she and Joel returned to the battlements and saw that General Fairfax had retreated a mile or two. The old ostler strained his keen countryman's eyes and said that it looked as though his soldiers were digging trenches and building forts.

"They're not going away? They're going to stay and besiege us?" she asked.

He nodded.

Then they looked nearer home. Far below them in Crouch Street, the Royalist burial parties were carrying away the bodies of the Parliament soldiers who had fallen fighting outside the walls.

Kate shivered again.

"Shall we go down to them?" she whispered.

Joel shook his head as he took her hand.

"Mr. Ryder, child . . . he . . . he'd be wantin' you to trust in the Lord. And trust we must. There's no other help."

A Terrible Grief

11

By that afternoon it was known in Colchester that General Fairfax had set up his headquarters close to Lexden parish church and was preparing for a long siege.

"Well, we can still march off north and east into Suffolk," Adam told Tamsin that night. "We only want time to tend our wounded and to round up new mounts."

"Dear Heaven," Kate prayed in silent anguish. "Please send them horses . . . so that Adam can ride away . . . ride away before he kills Father."

By eleven o'clock the next morning the streets were buzzing with the news that Fairfax had placed strong forces on all roads leading south and west out of the town and had urged the Suffolk trained bands to the north and east to guard the bridges over the Stour at Nayland and Stratford and Catawade.

"We've still got the Colne," Adam assured Tamsin. "We can still get supplies brought by sea up the river."

Yet, even here, he was immediately proved wrong. Next day an old Dutch merchant called upon Mrs.

Noordenbos and told her that the General had seized Mersea Island with its blockhouse. Pouncing with the swiftness of a cat, he had gained control of the river, too.

The investment was complete.

Kate saw that she had been right. The people of Colchester and their Royalist defenders were cut off from the outside world. They were caught like rats in a trap. Not even Uncle Ben and Ralph and the *Essex Maid* could come to their rescue.

Understanding her plight, she felt appalled. She was cut off from everyone she truly loved: from her father; from her mother; from Ralph. And, what was worse, she was afraid for them all. Achingly afraid. Her father might already have been killed. Her mother, alone and unprotected, might have had soldiers billeted on the farm as brutal and uncaring as those they had endured the year before. And as for Ralph, what generous, foolish thing might he not have done in this terrible predicament of war?

And where was her comfort here? She had Adam. She had Tamsin. She had the child. Adam was still Adam and Tamsin was still Tamsin. But they and the child were all in all to one another. They were complete. She felt herself alone, unwanted, a stranger standing outside a lighted window gazing in at their love.

And then, that same evening, coming back to St. Helen's Lane from the baker where she had stood for an hour for bread, she found that she was not alone.

Adam was waiting for her. He was sitting halfway up the stairs to the garret.

"Tamsin?" she asked in concern. "Where's Tamsin?"

"Nursing the child," he replied, raising his bandaged head from his hands.

"Does it hurt?" she asked quickly, seeing the pain in his face through the shadows. "Are you ill?"

He shook his head and drew her down beside him.

"Why did Mother let him go?" he asked in wretchedness.

"Father?"

"He's too old. He's much too old."

A little warmth came to her heart, knowing that her brother thought this, too.

"He'll be too stiff . . . too stiff for the fighting," Adam groaned. "He'll fall ill again of his fever . . ."

He saw it all, she thought. He saw how terrible it was for their father to be out there on Lexden Heath in arms against his son.

"*Why,* Kate? Why did he go? He must have known that I should be with Colonel Lucas?"

"Because he had to fight for what he thought was right," she replied bleakly.

"And so must I, Kate."

Gone was the pride and exultation of war.

"And so must I," he said again.

The words were wrung from him in agony.

She ached for him.

"I think Father understands," she murmured.

"And Mother? And Ralph?"

She did not know. But that Adam should care what they thought, that Adam, torn between his loyalty to the King and his love of his family, should feel so guilty and lost pulled at her heart. She sat on in the shadows at his side without speaking, overwhelmed with pity.

"I, too, have pledged myself," he said. "Kate . . . can *you* understand?"

Gone was the Adam whom as a child she had so childishly feared. She saw how that he was someone neither much older nor much wiser than Ralph or herself, someone far more bitterly distraught than either of them by the terror of the times.

Above them in the garret they heard Tamsin crooning to the child.

They were back in Colchester. In the siege.

She got to her feet, still clasping the two loaves of bread.

"You must go to them," she said gently. "Take them this loaf. I'll go down to Mrs. Noordenbos and give her this other one."

After this, she did what Joel had told her to do: she trusted in the Lord. The old ostler had been right: there was no other help. They were all shut up inside the beleaguered town and there was nothing that she or Tamsin or Joel or Mrs. Noordenbos or even that Adam could do about it. They had all better learn to endure whatever it was that they had to endure.

Yet, strangely enough, in those first days of the siege their trials were not great. There was more laughter to be heard in Colchester than tears. In the brief sunshine, she and Tamsin walked about the streets and watched the Royalist soldiers repairing the crumbling defenses; they were building sconces and ramparts and counterscarps and platforms all along the south and east and north walls of the town. This motley army, freed from the plow and dark workshop to fight for the King, were in holiday mood. They sang as they worked. For the moment, even the citizens were content to wait and hope for the best. It was as though everyone—like herself—had handed over his troubles to the Lord and had made peace with his brother.

But the sunshine did not last. Nor yet did their freedom from care.

Oddly as it seemed then, it was Tamsin who voiced the fear first.

"Kate," she said a day later as they watched the hundreds of soldiers at work on the walls. "How are we going to feed them all? Adam says that there are about four thousand of them—so he thinks. How shall we all have enough to eat, cooped up like this?"

Kate wondered too. The flour and butter and eggs and meat in the shops and stalls were already running out.

On the morrow, the Royalists found an answer. They plundered the merchants' warehouses at the Hythe and returned to the town with wagonloads of wheat, barley, rye, peas, and large quantities of salt fish.

"Here's something to give us a little cheer," said Adam that evening, putting down a small bag of wheat and a bottle of wine, and then pulling handfuls of raisins out of his pockets.

"Wine and raisins!" exclaimed Tamsin in delight.

They were luxuries unknown at Langby and High Ashfield.

"The merchants must have been storing up their goods for months," Adam said with a wan smile. "We never expected such a haul. And there was gunpowder, too. Barrels and barrels of it!"

"That's strange," said Kate, half smiling as she sipped the wine and put a few raisins into her mouth. "Uncle Ben might well have brought these upriver in the hold of the *Essex Maid.*"

And then, suddenly, her joy in the feast was gone. These were no stolen plums or meat pasty carefully slipped off their mother's larder shelf to be shared with Ralph. Such stolen pleasures had gone with their childhood.

Yet still the town and its garrison had to be fed.

In the early hours of June 22 she and Tamsin awoke to a great bleating and bellowing in High Street and the hallooing of horsemen driving stock. A large troop of cavaliers had slipped out under cover of dark and marauded the Hundred of Tending and driven a hundred sheep and sixty oxen back into the town.

"It's meat for nearly a week, Kate," said Adam shamefacedly that night when he heard her anger.

"But they're not *yours*—not your army's. They belong to poor farmers . . . like Father. You've robbed them, Adam. You've ruined them."

"The soldiers must eat," he said wretchedly. "Can't you see that they must eat?"

"They'll go to High Ashfield next!" she cried, aghast at the thought. "They'll go to Langby."

Next night the Royalist cavalry slipped out again, and Adam was ordered to ride with them. He knew the neighborhood too well not to be used as a guide.

That next evening he came to them more wretched still. He would not take Tamsin in his arms until he had blurted out the truth.

"I couldn't help it," he said miserably. "I tried to lead them off from your uncle's farm. But your brother Simon . . . he was waiting in the dark . . . at the crossroads beyond Wivenhoe. He was up on Challenge. He joined with us . . . and showed them the way."

"Simon!" exclaimed Tamsin, appalled.

"What've you taken?" Kate asked harshly.

"A dozen sheep . . . I think. And . . . and two milking cows."

"Poor Aunt Lucy," cried Tamsin, bursting into tears.

And it had all been for nothing, Adam went on bitterly, for one cow had stumbled into a ditch in the dark and broken her neck and the other had not been able to keep up with them. They had had to abandon her two miles this side of Wivenhoe.

"And Simon?" Kate asked disgustedly. "Did he ride back with you into the town?"

Adam shook his head. Simon had said that he could help the Royalist cause far better by staying where he was.

"He's a coward," she shouted. "A mean, traitorous coward. Next time he'll lead your thieving friends to Mother at High Ashfield."

She was so distraught by Simon's perfidy and her
mother's danger that she ran out of the attic and down
the stairs and with tears blurring her eyes fell straight
into Mrs. Noordenbos's arms.

"Poor child. Poor child," murmured the old woman,
leading her into her parlor. "Dis cruel var . . ."

Kate wiped her eyes. She was no child. And when
she had done so she saw that her old friend looked
distracted with grief herself.

Cruel, wicked news, Mrs. Noordenbos said, had just
come into town—brought by a member of Colonel
Cooke's Essex trained band who had deserted to the
Royalist cause.

"What news?" Kate asked, feeling faint. Colonel
Cooke was her father's commander.

"Dat General Fairfax . . . ee . . . 'as killed 'is
prisoners."

"*Killed* his prisoners!" she exclaimed incredulously.

There had been attempts on both sides to stop the
fighting, the old woman explained, but General Fairfax
and Lord Goring could not agree upon the terms of a
treaty. And the Parliament general, faced with an enemy
who would not surrender and fearing that at any
moment London and the rest of the country would rise in
support of the King, had ordered an example to be made.
He had decreed that among his prisoners every fifteenth
man of the Essex forces who was a bachelor and every
tenth married man should be shot. With the Londoners
and the men of Kent he had been even more savage.
Every fifth man was to be shot.

This sentence had been carried out four days
ago—on Monday, the 19th.

Kate sat there in the clean parlor with the rain
pouring down outside, shivering with horror.

"And de prisoners who are not killed," went on her
old friend, the tears rolling down her cheeks. "Dey are to
be . . . trans . . . transported over de sea."

There was a blue-and-white Delft jar on the table into which Mrs. Noordenbos had thrust four damask roses. Kate stared at the jar and smelled the sweet scent of the flowers, and sat on in silence, still staring, aghast at what the news meant for Adam. If General Fairfax took Colchester . . . then Adam . . . her brother Adam . . . she could not bear it . . . Adam might be put against the wall and shot . . . Adam might be sent in chains as a convict over the sea. The horror of it spread out and out like the pain from some dreadful wound . . . to Tamsin, to Abel, to her father and mother, to herself. The agony of Adam's fate engulfed them all.

The fate of the Royalist prisoners was known also to Adam.

"Promise me that you'll not tell Tamsin," he begged her that night as they stood together by their father's old horse.

Kate promised.

"And as for old Steadfast," he said wretchedly as he stroked their old friend's ears, "fodder's running out all over the town. When Joel's hay's gone, we'll have to let them slaughter him, Kate. There's nothing else we can do."

She swallowed hard as she nodded her head.

Throughout this dreadful time, it rained and rained. No one could remember so cold and stormy a June. The next afternoon Kate sat at the attic window staring out at the rain, wondering how her mother and Smy and old Bet and the hired man were managing about the hay in such a downpour. Behind her, Tamsin was crooning to her baby. It was not a happy sound. She was wrapped up in blankets and sat holding the child close to her body to keep them both warm. Two years ago, Kate thought as she listened to Tamsin's crooning, they had all been out mowing in the High Meadow—Ralph, Priscilla, Simon, Adam, Tamsin, and herself—all as merry as could be.

They had crowned the boys with flowers. They had all sung songs.

A great booming of guns suddenly brought her back to the present.

"Kate," gasped Tamsin, holding the baby tighter. "Whatever's that?"

The guns roared again, and they heard the crunch of cannonballs against stone. Soldiers shouted. A woman screamed. Kate stood up, opened the window, and put her head out into the rain and listened to the next salvo and the next and the next. Then she shut the window and sat down again.

"Well, what is it? What's happening?" Tamsin asked again.

"It's over by the North Gate," she replied.

How much should she tell Tamsin? Tamsin and the baby had not left the garret for the past few days because of the bad weather. She did not know that General Fairfax's army had advanced much closer to the town and had built forts—north, south, east, west—that one could see quite clearly as one stood on Head Hill. The one to the northwest by the North Gate was so close that the walls of the town were well within range of its cannon.

"But it's not near Adam?" Tamsin asked desperately, as the next salvo shook the window.

"No. He's to the south of the town. You know he is. He's guarding the outpost at Sir John Lucas's house."

"I know. I know. But I'm . . . I'm so frightened for him."

Tamsin's almost querulous fear made Kate glance at her again. She looked pinched, tired; there were dark circles under her eyes—and little wonder, for Abel had kept them both awake half the night, crying.

He started now again, the thin, reedy wail of the very young.

"He's ill, Kate. I'm sure he's ill," Tamsin burst out

frantically, clutching him closer as a tear began rolling down her cheek. "He never used to cry . . . never . . . not like this."

Outside, the booming of the guns had stopped.

"All babies cry," Kate replied sharply, knowing nothing about these things. "You're just tired. Give the baby to me. Go out for a little. Walk up and down in the lane."

"In the rain?"

"Well, go down to Mrs. Noordenbos. Just forget about Abel for half an hour."

When Tamsin had gone, Kate held her little nephew in her arms and looked down anxiously at his screwed-up face as he cried, wondering whether he was not looking a little pinched, too.

Tamsin must have burst out with her fears downstairs, for almost immediately the old Dutch woman climbed up to the attic and took Abel in her arms and rocked him and sang to him in her cracked old voice and so quieted the child.

"He must like the sound of Dutch," said Tamsin gratefully, with the wraith of a smile.

It was not songs that he wanted, the old woman told her. It was good mother's milk.

"Ven did you last eat, child?" she asked her.

"This morning . . . and again at noon."

They were not short of food, except milk. Adam had brought them the wheat and raisins and wine pillaged from the Hythe, and bread and a small Suffolk cheese from his army ration, and a leg of mutton from a sheep driven in from the country.

Their old friend shook her head. Then it was because Tamsin was frightened for her husband, she said. Her fear must be drying up her milk.

"Then what shall I *do?*" Tamsin asked, frantically.

"Dink only of de child. Only of de child," the old woman replied.

But how could Tamsin—or even Kate—think only of the child when its father was in such constant danger? For not only was Adam on duty all day in his outpost but—realizing that Tamsin must have food . . . and *good* food . . . if Abel were to survive—he now began slipping out of the East Gate under cover of dark, crossing the river, and marauding the nearby farms for anything he could easily carry away. One night he returned with a handful of early peas and a clutch of eggs; on the next he came back with a cockerel that he had knocked on the head. And Kate, who walked about the town during the day in the pouring rain and witnessed from the walls the near approach of the Suffolk trained bands from the east, knew that every night Adam's danger was the greater. One night her brother would get caught; he would not return.

And then, on July 1, came news that made her sigh with relief. Colonel Whalley, said the army spies, was erecting a strong battery in Greenstead churchyard close to the road running north and east into Suffolk. With Fairfax's forces now marshaled in strength between Adam and his farms, it was impossible for her brother to steal out into the countryside any more. She and Tamsin and Abel must take their luck with the rest of the people of Colchester.

Adam took the news grimly.

"Kate," he said to her as they walked up and down in the lane on the night of July 2, "you . . . you know that I may well be killed in the fighting . . . ?"

"Yes, Adam, I know," she murmured.

"And I may be gone . . . days . . . weeks . . . before this terrible siege is ended?"

She took his hand in the darkness. This, too, she had foreseen.

"Then . . . then you must help Tamsin and Abel
. . . to survive."

She promised. She loved them, she said. What else
would she want to do?

"But Adam, what can I *do?*" she asked miserably.
"It is impossible for me to do what you have done. I
cannot steal out into the country. The way is barred."

Adam shook his head. He did not know what she
could do, he said.

They parted sadly, he to his quarters and she back
to the attic. But before he left her, he took her in his arms
and kissed her on the forehead.

"You are a good girl, Kate. A brave girl. Tamsin
and Abel . . . they are all . . . all I have to leave to the
world. I leave them in your trust."

By July 4 Kate knew that the plight of the besieged
garrison was desperate. She could no longer climb to her
old vantage place in St. Mary's Church tower because
the soldiers had built a gun emplacement in the churchyard and civilians were forbidden to enter the whole
area. Yet there were wide views of the countryside from
all the walls of the town and, going the round of these
with Joel one morning, she was able to see clearly how
close Fairfax's army had approached to the Royalist
defenses. Beginning at the walls by the North Gate, they
looked across the orchards below the town walls at
Colonel Ingoldsby's Fort. It was so close that one could
see his musketeers walking about quite clearly; one could
almost read the expression on their faces.

"That's the closest they'n got to us, mawther," said
Joel. "Would to God t'others'd come up as smartly as ole
Ingoldsby."

And, over the Colne River, he pointed out to the
north, was the Rainborough Fort, and beyond that the
headquarters of the Suffolk regiment under Colonel
Fothergill. Walking along the north wall until the Castle

was behind them, they stopped and strained their eyes to see Fort Suffolk far away across the meadows to the northeast. Walking then along the east wall, they could see Colonel Whalley's Fort in Greenstead churchyard. To the south the distances were greater and the view was blurred by houses and by the great walls of the Lucas house and those of St. John's Abbey.

"Thet's where they'll attack, I've a mind," rumbled the old ostler. "Over there . . . out of sight . . . there's Colonel Fleetwood's horse, they say . . . an' . . . an' Colonel Needham's Tower regiment . . . an' all the forces under Colonel Barkstead an' Colonel Harlackenden . . . an' the ole Commander-in-Chief 'imself."

And that was where Adam was, thought Kate miserably, as she looked down on the suburbs to the south and on to the high roof and garden walls of Sir John Lucas's house.

Not knowing her fears, Joel gave her a slow Essex grin.

"Fairfax, Fleetwood, Whalley, Barkstead, Needham . . . Ingoldsby," he said, counting them on his fingers. "Why, we un get the whole lot on un out there . . . tryin' to set us free."

Kate knew what he meant. She had heard the drum roll of these names all her life. Ralph had treasured them proudly. They were the great heroes of the Parliament army.

In spite of her fear for Adam, she responded to the call.

"And there's my father out there, too," she flashed back at him, with something akin to pride.

Adam said that the Royalists, too, expected that Fairfax's attack would come from the south, for the Parliament pioneers had begun to build earthworks even closer to the south walls.

"We've done what we can to harry their engineers,"

Adam told Tamsin and Kate on the night of the 10th. "We've managed to haul a saker up onto the belfry platform of St. Mary's Church."

"A *saker!*" Kate exclaimed, thinking how heavy a cannon must be to pull up to such a height.

"And we've got a splendid one-eyed gunner," he went on. "A true marksman—who picks off their pioneers as they build their new battery."

Thank God her father would not be one of the pioneers, she thought. He was too old. Too distinguished a campaigner. They would never set him to digging trenches.

No one could doubt any longer that the main attack was going to come from the south. Yet it was delayed two days further because of a strange mistake made by the Parliament engineers. When their artillerymen came to fire from the battery on the morning of the 12th, they found that St. Mary's Church and its saker and the Royal Fort on the Balkon were both beyond their range. The Royalist defenders shouted in derision; but an hour later—no longer mocking—they were forced to watch their enemy building new earthworks and new gun emplacements even nearer to the south wall.

At sunset on Thursday, July 13, Adam came to them in the attic. He looked hollow-eyed with watching, but was both resolute and calm.

"They will attack on the morrow," he told them. "I will come to you again when I can . . ."

He kissed Kate on the forehead and bade her go down to sit with Mrs. Noordenbos.

At dawn on the 14th she and Tamsin awoke to the first salvo of Fairfax's advance battery. The windows rattled. Abel cried and Tamsin ran to his cradle.

The onslaught had begun.

Kate sat in one corner of the garret watching Tamsin clutching Abel in another and listened to the thudding of the guns, praying that the town would fall quickly; that Adam would somehow escape or be pardoned; and that their father would come and take them all away to the quietness of home. Yet on and on thundered the culverins and drakes, and on and on came the brutal crunch of cannonball against masonry and the rattle of musketry and the cries of hurt soldiers and the screams of women and children.

At last, she could bear Tamsin's tortured face no longer.

"You are safe, here . . . both of you," she said hurriedly. "I'll go down to Joel . . . just for a minute. I'll be back . . . and I'll tell you what he says."

She met Joel in the lane.

"They've hit St. Mary's Church," he burst out. "Tumbled down tower . . . an' bells . . . an' all."

"And the saker?"

Joel nodded. The saker had come crashing down with the bells.

"An' our wool . . . great bales on it," he shouted through another deafening roar from the guns. "Our wool, it's burnin' all along the Lucas garden walls."

"*Wool?*" she exclaimed incredulously, though even as she spoke she could smell the burning bales in the south wind.

The defenders, he told her, were stuffing the breaches made in the walls with anything they could lay their hands on. In Colchester, this meant wool.

"And the fighting?" she asked, gulping hard, knowing that she felt sick at heart whichever way the fighting was going.

"Sallies and counter-sallies," he shouted over the screech of war.

"Thrust of pike . . . hand to hand . . . this way and that."

"And all around Sir John Lucas's house?"

He nodded his head. That was what their Parlia-

ment friends had a mind to take, he told her sorrowfully, knowing at last that her brother was stationed there.

"And Colonel Whalley's crossed the river to the east and taken the Hythe," he said.

"The Hythe?"

They were attacked on all sides.

When she returned to the weaver's house, she found that Mrs. Noordenbos had got Tamsin and Abel down with her in her parlor. The old woman was pouring her out a cordial from a little stone jar. As she came into the room, Tamsin shook her head.

"Adam . . . Adam . . . is fighting . . . is fighting for his life," she said slowly.

She spoke as though she were in a trance, as though she were not sitting there quietly in Mrs. Noordenbos's parlor with Abel in her arms, but as though she were at Adam's side by that terrible garden wall.

Late in the afternoon, there came a lull.

"Is it at an end?" Tamsin whispered.

"I will go and see," Kate said, knowing that there was nothing more she could do for Tamsin. Tamsin had passed into a world beyond her reach.

She ran out of St. Helen's Lane and into High Street and asked the first townsman she met.

"How is it? What's happening?"

"The garden walls are down," he replied. "Barkstead's and Ewer's men are making the final assault."

She ran on into Head Street and stood among the crowd of townspeople on the height, looking down toward the fighting. Soldiers were standing on the walls on either side of Head Gate, shouting back the news.

"They're in! They're in!"

"No. The garrison's still fighting."

"They're making a brave stand," said a weaver quite close to her. "They've fought like . . . like lions."

It was all over, she thought in anguish. Adam must be dead or else taken prisoner.

"Barkstead's men are sacking the house," came another voice.

And then, out of the hubbub, came a triumphant yell.

"They've got away," bawled a soldier. "The garrison's slipped away into St. John's Abbey!"

Kate ran back down Cornhill and High Street and burst into Mrs. Noordenbos's parlor.

"They've got away, Tamsin," she shouted. "Adam and his friends have given them the slip . . ."

The garrison at the Lucas house, she said, had

managed to fight their way to the other fortified outpost on the southern perimeter. They were now safe in St. John's Abbey.

It was only a night and a morning's respite for them both.

At three o'clock on the afternoon of the 15th, Fairfax threw in a fresh assault party consisting of musketeers and troops with scaling ladders to capture the citadel of the Abbey. The fighting was even fiercer and bloodier than the day before.

At five o'clock a huge explosion rocked the town.

"God, what can have happened?" Kate exclaimed aloud, as the Delft jar with the roses fell off Mrs. Noordenbos's table.

Tamsin had clutched the baby so wildly that he was howling with fright.

"Go and see, Kate," said the old woman.

Out in High Street she learned that a fire ball had landed in the Royalist powder magazine. The defenders of the Abbey were now fighting their way back through the suburbs into Colchester itself.

"An' they're settin' fire to the houses," wept a woman in anguish.

"*Our* houses. They're throwin' in brands . . . an' settin' em all alight."

That night Kate and Tamsin lay in the garret, watching the red clouds of smoke passing over the night sky and smelling the terrible stench of burned wool and wood and thatch.

Adam had not come back to them.

"Kate," whispered Tamsin in the lurid darkness. "He cannot have lived through this dreadful day."

Kate jumped up and lay down beside her, trying to buoy her with hope. Adam might be wounded, she said—or taken prisoner. Or he might just have been kept by his lieutenant from coming home to them.

Soon after dawn, Kate awoke to find her friend kneeling in prayer beside the cradle.

"Tamsin?"

She turned her face. It was calm and beautiful in its terrible grief.

"Adam died an hour ago," she said quietly. "I know it, Kate. He . . . he told me so."

"Think Only of the Child"

12

The next noontide, a fellow soldier, a friend of Adam's, came to them in St. Helen's Lane with the news of his death engraved on his pale, worn face. Adam was dead, he said. He had been mortally wounded by a pike-thrust through his chest while defending the great Gatehouse of the Abbey. He and his companions had been forced to leave him there, propped up against the Gatehouse wall, when they had fought their rearguard action back through the southern suburbs into the town.

"Then, you do not know," Kate burst out. "He may still be alive."

The young volunteer shook his head.

No. One of the citizens of Colchester, he said, who had stayed behind near the Abbey to get the furniture out of his burning house, had been driven back into the town this morning by Fairfax's soldiers and had told their commanding officer that the young infantryman propped up against the Gatehouse wall had died in the night.

"May the Lord receive him," said Tamsin quietly, making the sign of the cross and bowing her head.

"He fought bravely, did your man," blurted out the young recruit.

"Of *course* he fought bravely!" Kate rapped out.

In the long hours of that afternoon and evening and night, she wondered how she could reach Tamsin in her frozen resignation. She too had lost Adam; she had lost a brother. But Tamsin had lost the light of her life. She knew that she was shut out by her friend's grief—just as she had been shut out by her love. She was standing outside the window again, looking sadly into a darkened room.

Next morning, it was Abel—not herself—who melted his mother's grief.

"Tamsin," said the old widow, when she brought

her up a bowl of hot oaten gruel. "You must rouse yourself . . . get vell again. De child needs you."

Back down in her parlor, she told Kate roundly that there was no milk to be had in the whole of Colchester. If Tamsin did not rouse herself and recover her health, she might lose the baby, too. She must have fresh air. She must walk out in the open. Then she must sleep.

"Take Tamsin down by de castle, Kate . . . by de river. I vill mind de child."

The fighting had died down with the taking of the Gatehouse. But there had come no surrender. The Royalist defenders were repairing the walls. The siege was going on.

As the two of them walked out into the sunshine on that quiet Monday morning Kate wondered desperately if it was ever going to end.

Fearing the worst, she had borrowed a sack from Mrs. Noordenbos.

"What do you want that sack for?" Tamsin asked listlessly, as they turned left into High Street and then immediately left again into the green meadowland about the castle.

"For forage."

"Forage?"

For Steadfast, she explained. Joel had stolen hay from the Royalists' store of forage and so kept the old horse alive up till now. But they had now set a guard on their loft.

"He says I should gather grass around by the castle," she went on, "and pull leaves from the trees . . . and . . . and anything else I can think of. It's what the troopers are doing themselves, he said."

When they had walked well into the meadowland, they found that they were almost too late. Horses were picketed everywhere under the trees; the grass was close cropped and what had not already been eaten was bruised and muddied, the ground being soggy from the late heavy rains.

"Right up under the walls it's not so bad," said Tamsin, rousing herself a little. "And look, Kate . . . look at all those clumps of flowers growing high up inside the cracks."

No one had thought of the valerian and the stone crops and the thin grasses sprouting out of the castle walls. Sadly, with their grief sore in their hearts, they picked any green, living thing they could reach and then walked on toward the north wall of the town, pulling leaves from the lower branches of the trees as they went. Once up on the wall, they looked across the tenting ground and the water meadows at the swollen river, its waters flashing in the sunlight. Here, north of Colchester, the Colne coursed in a great half circle, turning abruptly south away to their right and then, after passing under the East Bridge, turning east again, until it turned south once more to flow under the bridge upstream from the Hythe.

Kate gazed in silence at the swollen river, knowing that it was *their* river: Adam's and Ralph's and her own; that it flowed under their jetty at High Ashfield.

Tamsin, beside her, gave a little shiver. She, too, was gazing at the river.

"We're so close to your mother, Kate, by the river," she said sadly. "So close . . . and . . . and such a long way off."

The thought of her mother brought peace to Kate. But to Tamsin it brought anguish.

"Kate," she burst out, suddenly distraught. "She'll never forgive us for Adam's death. She'll never forgive Abel and me for what we've done."

Kate gazed at her in amazement and then threw down the sack and ran to her. Adam's death was none of their doing, she said. And Abel was Adam's son. His *son*.

163

Her mother would love and treasure him to the end of her days. And as for Tamsin herself, she was Adam's wife. She had given him love. Her mother would love Tamsin as she loved her child.

Back in the garret, Tamsin held Abel in her arms and at last burst into tears.

"Yes," she said over and over again. "He is Adam's son."

In the week that followed Adam's death, a sad sort of peace came to them both. For Tamsin, the terror was over. There was no Adam to watch for any longer, to wait for, to fear for. There was no husband to wake for in anguish in the middle of the night. And since all was at an end for him, she gave herself up to his son.

"Kate," she murmured in sad wonder one evening. "Is it not strange, my milk is coming better. The child has enough. Look, he is smiling . . . smiling at us both."

For Kate, it was the calm of being certain of what she must do. As the siege wore on and food grew scarcer in the shops, she saw that she must go on plundering for themselves—as well as for Steadfast. She had given Adam her promise. She would save Tamsin and Abel, come what come may. She would steal for them, fight for them, die for them. She was quite clear in her mind what she must do. And the clearness brought her peace.

On Friday, July 21, while she was out walking with her sack in the meadowland just inside the north wall of the town, a shower of arrows sailed over her head with a piece of paper attached to each shaft. One of the arrows fell at her feet. She tore off the paper and read General Fairfax's offer of money and a pardon to any common soldier who deserted from Lord Goring. At first, she could hardly believe what she read. Then, seeing two Royalist officers running toward the fallen arrows to destroy the free pardons, she stuffed the paper down into the sack with the bits of grass and walked on.

On the way home, she felt bitterly angry at Adam's hard fate. Had he lived till today, she thought, he could have saved his life. He could have slipped out of the town under cover of dark, swum the river, and crept home to High Ashfield. Their mother would have loved him, comforted him, tried to give him back his peace of mind.

Then she came to herself with a jolt. Adam would never have deserted his wife and his child—and his cause.

When she returned to the attic, his last gift to them stood there beside the food bin, a bushel of barley—stolen from goodness knows where. It was the only food now left to them—and it was a silent and terrible rebuke to her.

And now began a horrible time for the beleaguered town.

The next day, Saturday, July 22, the Royalist Council of War ordered all the cavalry horses to be drawn up in the great ditch surrounding the castle.

Kate and Tamsin and Mrs. Noordenbos stood at the head of the lane watching the troopers riding their horses along High Street, wondering what was afoot now. In less than an hour, they knew. Each third horse had been handed over to the army cooks for slaughter, either to be eaten straightaway or else to be powdered for future food.

That night Joel came to them with tears running down his cheeks. The Commissariat had seized Steadfast. There had been nothing he could do to stop them.

Kate tried to comfort him. He had done his best. She was sure he had done his best. Yet, she wept herself. She could not bear to think of her old friend being dragged off and killed by an army cook.

Next day, with no forage to gather, she sat sadly at home mourning Steadfast and thinking, unaccountably, of the joys of her mother's larder: the cheeses and dumplings and the raised rabbit pies. That night her feet and her chest were cold and she felt odd little stabbing pains in her stomach.

On the morrow, she felt better. Mrs. Noordenbos brought them up four thick slices of grilled bacon, a half loaf of rye bread, and a crock of home-brewed ale.

"But we cannot take your food," they both protested.

She was an old woman, she replied. She had not a stomach for food . . . not like the young.

"But see," said Kate, "we still have Adam's barley."

Then keep it, she was told. They might all need Adam's barley by the end of the week . . . and the rest of the smoked bacon in her chimney and the ale . . . and the peck of rye flour she had hidden away in a stone crock.

"Then we will share what we have?" Kate asked.

The old Dutchwoman nodded her head. Then she turned to Tamsin. Could she, for her part, she asked shyly, share a little in the joy of the child?

Tamsin—with tears in her eyes—stooped down, picked Abel out of his cradle, and put him gently into her arms.

Each of them understood that it was a bond sealed between them.

Daily and hourly both defenders and townspeople expected the final assault.

"Father will be here today, tomorrow, Wednesday, Thursday," Kate told herself, counting off the days on her hands.

Yet the days and the hours dragged by and the food within the town dwindled to the scrapings of bins and sacks—and still no storming came.

On Tuesday, July 25, Colonel Rainborough's forces made an attack to the north and destroyed the town's last remaining corn mill.

"Why a *mill?*" Kate asked Joel, much puzzled. "Why didn't they come on through the gates and deliver us all?"

The older ostler sighed wearily. He looked pale and drawn.

"I've a mind, mawther," he replied, fixing her with lackluster eyes. "I've a mind Fairfax . . . he's figured on *starving* them out."

"But that means starving *us*," she exclaimed.

"Aye, mawther, it do."

That night Kate looked at Tamsin bending over Abel as she nursed him and took a tight hold of her courage. Half of Mrs. Noordenbos's rye had already gone and the whole of the bacon. And they had dipped into Adam's barley.

On August 2, she committed her first act of theft.

Earlier in the day, the Council had ordered a second rendezvous of the garrison's horses, and the fattest of these were picked out and given over to the cooks. The cavalier officers billeted in the George Inn, however, had kept back a fat little pony for themselves.

That night they roasted it whole in the inn yard.

She and Tamsin, sitting by the cradle at the attic window, could see the glow of the fire in the sky across the lane and smell the smell of the roasting flesh.

It was more than either of them could bear.

"If we had just a little, little piece . . . just . . . just a very, very little piece," Tamsin sighed.

Kate glanced across at her. She looked haggard. Abel had begun crying again both at night and by day. Her milk must be failing.

She jumped up, resolved.

"Lend me your dark cloak," she demanded.

"Kate . . . Kate . . . what are you going to do?" Tamsin called after her as she ran down the stairs.

Once out in the fire-flecked darkness of the lane, she stopped to think out the best way of getting some of the meat. Should she creep in through the yard gate behind some swaggering officer and hope that no one saw her? Go around to the front of the inn—to the taproom—and mingle with the servants? Or walk boldly into the yard and demand to see the ostler?

She decided on the last.

When it came to it, there was no need to ask for Joel. The officers were drunk and not one of them noticed her, clad in her dark cloak. They were swilling the last of the wine that they had plundered from the Hythe; they were laughing and shouting as they cut the flesh with their daggers. Their hands were gleaming with blood. She stood there in the shadows by Steadfast's old stall, watching them, sick with disgust. And then she smelled again the rich smell of the roasting meat and felt again her great craving for food—and knew that she was quite as human as these men were.

Suddenly, she saw her chance.

One young cavalry officer, more drunk than the rest, had cut his pound of flesh from the roasted pony and had it speared on his dagger. As he swayed from the heat of the fire to eat it, the meat dropped from its point. She was in among the boots and spurs in a moment, as swift as a cat. And away she fled, panic-stricken and gasping, this way and that in the shadows, the roar of voices in her ears, and as she reached the gate, a hand clutching at Tamsin's mantle. She gave a desperate twist to her body and left the cloak behind in the man's hand and ran on into the dark lane in her pale dress, sobbing, clutching the hot meat to her chest.

"It's a maid," shouted one of the roisterers in tipsy delight. "Fletcher, you've lost your meat to a maid!"

Shouts of laughter rose from the inn yard.

She stumbled up the stairs to the attic, triumphant but still sobbing. She was a thief. A thief. She had broken the eighth commandment.

"Kate!" gasped Tamsin, as she stood there, holding the bloody meat.

"Just a little . . . only just a little for tonight," she panted. "Just a mouthful."

Next morning Mrs. Noordenbos sent her out to pick cresses and dandelion leaves from the town walls.

"I vill make a stew," she told them.

With a pint of Adam's barley and the herbs and a pan of water, she could make a stew with the horsemeat, she said, that might last them for three days.

That same day, the Royalists themselves dispensed with the eighth commandment. On that August 3, they searched the inhabitants' houses and took away all their billhooks.

Kate and Tamsin watched the infantrymen marching up and down High Street, humorously shouldering their new arms.

Four days later they went into action, sallying out of all the five gates of the town in yet another futile attempt to break out of Fairfax's encirclement.

"When will it ever end?" Kate asked in despair on the evening of August 8. "When will Father ever come to take us away?"

She was alone with Mrs. Noordenbos in the parlor below. Though they had husbanded their stocks as carefully as they could, they had less than half of Adam's barley left, a small cheese, which their old neighbor had bought at great cost from a fellow Dutchwoman, and a handful of the rye.

Upstairs, she had left Abel wailing and wailing for his mother's milk. Unless they could get Tamsin more food, the baby would die.

The child's thin cries came down to them in the parlor.

Mrs. Noordenbos frowned as she listened and then rose and beckoned Kate into her dairy.

"Look, Kate," she said, pointing to a small earthenware pot covered with a lid. "I 'ave kept dis for dem . . . for Tamsin and de child. Look."

She shifted the lid and showed her its contents.

"Honey?" Kate asked.

The old woman nodded.

If they boiled water and put in a spoonful of honey, they could keep mother and child alive for three days, perhaps four . . . perhaps longer. She did not know.

Wearily, and with the numbness of starvation slowly dulling their minds, the three of them lived through the next terrible week.

The whole town was in distress. The greatest

distress. There was no horseflesh left. The soldiers—and the townsfolk, too—were killing the dogs and cats.

One morning Kate and Mrs. Noordenbos were sitting in the parlor window, idly watching a soldier tempting a stray dog into his reach with a pellet of bread.

"It's awful. I can't bear it," Kate gulped, thinking of Polly and turning away as the dog responded and the soldier grabbed it by the throat.

The old woman beside her, however, merely nodded her head. It had given her an idea, she murmured.

That same afternoon, she called excitedly up the attic stairs.

"Kate . . . Tamsin . . . come quick. I . . . I . . . 'ave caught a pigeon."

On August 16, driven desperate by their hunger, many women, with their children hanging to their skirts, clamored in front of Lord Goring's headquarters to let them go out of the town.

An hour later, Kate and Tamsin and Mrs. Noordenbos took Abel with them up onto the battlements and stood among the crowd, watching a woman with five children walk out of the town toward General Fairfax's sentinel.

"Look," cried Tamsin in anguish. "Look. The soldiers are bringing them back."

There was no hope for any of them, Kate thought in despair. No hope, from either friend or foe.

"Courage," their neighbor whispered in her ear. "I 'ave caught anudder two pigeons."

And then came their final ordeal.

On August 21, Lord Goring ordered a search for food for his soldiers to be made in every house in the town.

When they came to the little house in St. Helen's Lane, there was so little barley meal left in the bin that the officer in charge of the search party left them with what they had. But, going into the dairy, he found the honey.

"Honey?" said the young man, licking his fingers. "Well, we'll leave you with your barley meal . . . but we'll take this."

"No!" cried Tamsin in despair.

"No!" cried Mrs. Noordenbos.

Kate, stupid though she was from lack of food, thought quickly what to do.

"Let him take it," she said to them. "See, I will give it to you myself."

And, picking up the little earthenware pot, she let it fall bang on the floor.

"You fool," he yelled, slapping her across the face. "Look what you've done!"

When he had gone, the three of them stood and stared at the honey spilled out among the bits of earthenware on the tiles.

"You did it on purpose!" Tamsin exclaimed aghast. "*Why?* Why?"

The floor was clean, Kate snapped as she knelt down to pick out the bits of broken jar. They could soon spoon the honey back into another pot.

A long five days later, hope came to them at last. On Saturday, August 26, Lord Goring sent messengers out of the town to ask for General Fairfax's terms of surrender. Very early in the morning of the Monday following, the beleaguered garrison assembled in different quarters of the town to lay down their arms. And at ten o'clock Colonel Rainsborough and the Tower regiment entered Colchester through the North Gate and Colonel Ingoldsby by the Head Gate.

The eleven weeks' siege of Colchester was over.

At dusk, her father had them both in his arms.

Home Again

13

All to do, thought Kate a fortnight later, as she stood high up in an apple tree gazing at the sunlight winking everywhere in the standing pools and at her father raking out the rotten wheat-straw from the seven-acre field. "Thank God there's all to do!"

With the ceaseless rain of the past two months, the crops had rotted where they stood. Wheat, barley, apricots, plums, all had been lost.

Her father raised his head as she watched him and smiled in her direction.

"Those apples can scarce be worth the picking," he called out to her.

"They're good enough for me," she called back, pulling one down from above her head and burying her teeth in its flesh.

Everything was good enough for her. Everything was golden: the puddles, the rotten wheat, the sweet smells, the blackberries, the hard work, Polly looking up at her from the foot of the tree. After the anguish of

Adam's death and the horrors of the siege, she wanted to lap herself around, bury herself fathoms deep in all that belonged to High Ashfield.

"Shake the rotten ones down," her father shouted. "The pigs might have joy of them." It was a trick Ralph had taught her long ago.

And thinking of Ralph, she was filled with quiet content. He was still left to her. The old Ralph. He had not been changed by the war.

Ralph had been here at the farm when they came home. He and Uncle Ben, denied harborage for the *Essex Maid* at the Hythe during the siege, had moored the hoy at the end of the jetty and had given her mother what comfort and help they could. He must have seen the three of them: Tamsin and herself and their father, carrying Abel, trailing wearily down the lane, for he had raced up to meet them, shouting his joy, with Polly barking and crying out at his heels.

"Father! Kate! Tamsin!"

And then, he had stopped, his face clouded with fear.

There had been no Adam for him to greet.

"He died bravely," Tamsin had told Kate's mother the first night that they were home. "He died for what he thought was right."

She had said it in defiance.

But there had been no need.

"I know that he died bravely," Kate's father had replied, taking Tamsin's hand lovingly in his own. "I saw where our son had his wounds."

"You *saw* . . . " Kate had exclaimed.

He had been ordered to the Gatehouse of the Abbey, he said, soon after dawn on July 16.

"I found his body by the wall. The pike-thrust had gone in through his breast. He had not received that wound in running away."

Kate, up her apple tree, stopped swinging the branches about and thought long about the grief that had come to them all in Adam's death.

Her mother had not railed against fate or turned upon Tamsin and her child. She had taken both to her heart. But Kate saw that it was a bruised heart that her mother had and that it was a bewildered, inconsolable grief that she tried to keep hidden. She had lost Adam, her firstborn, her favorite child. Now that he had died—died with honor—he would stay there forever, the closest in love of them all.

As for Tamsin, coming back to High Ashfield had only increased the sharpness of her pain. Every room in the house, every field, every lane spoke to her of Adam and reminded her of her loss.

Yet, she had his son. She was brave.

That morning she had taken over the dairy work and begun to make butter.

Kate saw that her father, dazed too by his loss, was seeking comfort in his grandson. Abel was now six months old and was fast recovering from his ordeal.

Last night her father had carried him on his shoulder around the farm.

"It'll all be his, Kate," he had told her as they walked up to the High Meadow. "Abel'll live on after us here on my father's farm."

She had looked up at the boy clutching at his grandfather's white hair. In spite of Tamsin's dark eyes, he was all Ryder, she thought.

It was right and good, her father had said. It was right and good that his grandson should live in the house that his own father had built and pick the apples from the trees that his father had planted.

"The land is a bond that seals all, Kate," he said. "Adam saved High Ashfield for me. Now it is my task to save it for Abel."

Yes, Slowly, slowly, we shall recover ourselves, she thought sadly as she climbed down out of the apple tree.

Yet, so strange and cruel is war, that before that month of September was out, they were all thanking God that Adam had died as he had.

It was poor Ralph who brought them the news.

Kate was helping her father with the rotten wheat at the time when, looking up, she saw Ralph running up toward them from the jetty.

"Father, Father," he burst out, distraught with his tidings. "They said . . . they said they'd pardon the common soldiers."

"And now?"

"They're sending them off in chains . . . to Bristol. They're going to . . . to transport them as . . . as convicts."

Her father passed his hand over his eyes and then leaned on his rake handle in silent prayer.

"God help us all," he said at last. "God help us Englishmen that we should have come to this."

God's Englishmen had not yet finished with their vengeance.

Four months later they led their anointed King—Adam's King—out through a window in Whitehall onto a scaffold and chopped off his head.

The wounds of the terrible war took long to heal. But looking back a year later, Kate saw for herself that they healed quickest where love had always been stronger than hate. Here with them at High Ashfield, the pain of the times slowly died to a throb and then to an ache. And, at length, it settled to a sadness that came to them suddenly after laughter—a sorrowful remembrance of other days and of Adam, the young father of the child growing to boyhood in their midst.

She and Tamsin sang their old songs together; and

Tamsin romped with her child. But at the end of the day Kate saw that the darkness had come back into her friend's mind.

"Tamsin will marry again," her father had once said to her. "She is too full of life and happiness not to wed."

But Kate had shaken her head.

"I can never forget Adam. Never," Tamsin had blurted out to her as they bound the sheaves that first harvest after his death. "How could I live with another man—after loving Adam?"

As for herself, peace came to her in a daily thankfulness that she was safely back home doing her humdrum tasks on the farm, surrounded by Tamsin and her family, and once a week visiting Mrs. Noordenbos and Joel, her old friends in Colchester. She knew only that she loved the changing seasons as they came to field and hedge and copse . . . and that she still loved looking down from the High Meadow on the River Colne and watching the ships sailing up to the Hythe.

In her thankfulness, she asked for no more.

But no one can stay still, least of all when one is young.

"Goodness, Kate, you look almost pretty!" Ralph burst out in surprise one day a few months later.

"Pretty?" she exclaimed in astonishment. "Why, what's different?"

"I . . . I don't know," he replied, puzzled. "You don't look like a pony, any more . . . a pony that's been rolling itself in the grass."

Six months later, her mother commended the quality of her yarn and told her now that she was nearly sixteen they had better begin laying aside their profits from the yarn sales in order to purchase her dowry sheets.

"Dowry sheets?" she asked, in wonder.

Had it come to that?

"Why," exclaimed Tamsin, laughing, "do you not know that you are to go to your husband with more sheets and coverlids and bed hangings and mattresses than was ever heard of in the whole of Essex?"

A husband?

"And who shall I bring home to you, my dear daughter?" asked her father a year later. "A rich man . . . like Mr. Smedley . . . if I can get him? A grave, religious man . . . like Mr. Pratt? Or a man, Kate, to take Ralph's place and sail away with you to America?"

She laughed and shook her head.

Then she sat silent for a little, trying to frame the words to express her heart's desire.

"Go and bring me back a man . . . a man like yourself, Father," she said at last. "And . . . and like Adam . . . and Ralph."

And then she paused and felt anxious.

"And please, Father, let him be living near High Ashfield . . . not . . . not . . . not more than a day's ride away from you all."

∾ *About the Author*

Hester Burton is a distinguished novelist known on both sides of the Atlantic for her rare ability to re-create the past in vivid and memorable terms. She won the Carnegie Medal in England for *Time of Trial; Beyond the Weir Bridge* and *The Rebel* were chosen as Notable Books of 1971/1972 respectively by the American Library Association; and she has received many other honors and awards for her writing. An Oxford graduate herself, Mrs. Burton is married to an Oxford don, a classicist who shares her interest in history.

∾ *About the Illustrator*

Victor G. Ambrus lives in Hampshire, England, near Basingstoke and Reading. He describes the countryside as "real civil war country, where every other village inn or church still bears bullet holes and other relics of Cromwell's troops." He particularly enjoyed doing the illustrations for *Kate Ryder*, which takes place in this period—a favorite period for Mr. Ambrus.

Born in Budapest, Victor Ambrus left Hungary after the 1956 uprisings and continued his studies at the Royal College of Art in London. He has illustrated many children's books, and received the British Library Association's Kate Greenaway Medal for his outstanding illustrations.

F
BUR

Burton, Hester
Kate Ryder

DATE			